The Pirates of Panama

Or

The Buccaneers of America

A True Account of the Famous Adventures and Daring Deeds of Sir Henry Morgan and Other Notorious Freebooters of the Spanish Main

By Alexander O. Exquemelin

Published by Pantianos Classics

ISBN-13: 978-1537698625

First published in 1678

This edition was first published in 1914

A Buccaneer Upon a Tropical Island

Contents

Introduction

This volume was originally written in Dutch by John Esquemeling, and first published in Amsterdam in 1678 under the title of De Americaeneche Zee Roovers. It immediately became very popular and this first hand history of the Buccaneers of America was soon translated into the principal European languages. The first English edition was printed in 1684.

Of the author, John Esquemeling, very little is known although it is generally conceded that he was in all probability a Fleming or Hollander, a quite natural supposition as his first works were written in the Dutch language. He came to the island of Tortuga, the headquarters of the Buccaneers, in 1666 in the employ of the French West India Company. Several years later this same company, owing to unsuccessful business arrangements, recalled their representatives to France and gave their officers orders to sell the company's land and all its servants. Esquemeling then a servant of the company was sold to a stern master by whom he was treated with great cruelty. Owing to hard work, poor food and exposure he became dangerously ill, and his master seeing his weak condition and fearing to lose the money Esquemeling had cost him resold him to a surgeon. This new master treated him kindly so that Esquemeling's health was speedily restored, and after one year's service he was set at liberty upon a promise to pay his benefactor, the surgeon, 100 pieces of eight at such a time as he found himself in funds.

Once more a free man he determined to join the pirates and was received into their society and remained with them until 1672. Esquemeling served the Buccaneers in the capacity of barber-surgeon, and was present at all their exploits. Little did he suspect that his first hand observations would some day be cherished as the only authentic and true history of the Buccaneers and Marooners of the Spanish Main.

From time to time new editions of this work have been published, but in many cases much new material, not always authentic, has been added and the result has been to mar the original narrative as set forth by Esquemeling. In arranging this edition, the original English text only has been used, and but few changes made by cutting out the long and tedious description of plant and animal life of the West Indies of which Esquemeling had only a smattering of truth. But, the history of Captain Morgan and his fellow buccaneers is here printed almost identical with the original English translation, and we believe it is the first time this history has been published in a suitable form for the juvenile reader with no loss of interest to the adult.

The world wide attention at this time in the Isthmus of Panama and the great canal connecting the Atlantic with the Pacific Ocean lends to this narrative an additional stimulus. Here are set forth the deeds of daring of the wild freebooters in crossing the isthmus to attack the cities, Puerto Bellow and Panama. The sacking and burning of these places accompanied by pillage, fire, and treasure seeking both on land and on sea form exciting reading. The Buccaneers and Marooners of America well deserves a place on the book shelf with those old world-wide favorites Robinson Crusoe and the Swiss Family Robinson.

George Alfred Williams

The Translator to the Reader (of 1684)

THE present Volume, both for its Curiosity and Ingenuity, I dare recommend unto the perusal of our English nation, whose glorious actions it containeth. What relateth unto the curiosity hereof, this Piece, both of Natural and Humane History, was no sooner published in the Dutch Original, than it was snatch't up for the most curious Library's of Holland; it was Translated into Spanish (two impressions thereof being sent into Spain in one year); it was taken notice of by the learned Academy of Paris; and finally recommended as worthy our esteem, by the ingenious Author of the Weekly Memorials for the Ingenious, printed here at London about two years ago. Neither all this undeservedly, seeing it enlargeth our acquaintance of Natural History, so much prized and enquir'd for, by the Learned of this present Age, with several observations not easily to be found in other accounts already received from America: and besides, it informeth us (with huge novelty) of as great and bold attempts, in point of Military conduct and valour, as ever were performed by mankind; without excepting, here, either Alexander the Great, or Julius Cæsar, or the rest of the Nine Worthy's of Fame. Of all which actions, as we cannot confess ourselves to have been ignorant hitherto (the very name of Bucaniers being, as yet, known but unto few of the Ingenious; as their Lives, Laws, and Conversation, are in a manner unto none) so can they not choose but be admired, out of this ingenuous Author, by whosoever is curious to learn the various revolutions of humane affairs. But, more especially by our English Nation; as unto whom these things more narrowly do appertain. We having here more than half the Book filled with the unparallel'd, if not inimitable, adventures and Heroick exploits of our own Country-men, and Relations; whose undaunted, and exemplary courage, when called upon by our King and Country, we ought to emulate.

From whence it hath proceeded, that nothing of this kind was ever, as yet, published in England, I cannot easily determine; except, as some will say, from some secret Ragion di Stato. Let the reason be as t'will;

this is certain, so much the more we are obliged unto this present Author, who though a stranger unto our Nation, yet with that Candour and Fidelity hath recorded our Actions, as to render the Metal of our true English Valour to be the more believed and feared abroad, than if these things had been divulged by our selves at home. From hence peradventure will other Nations learn, that the English people are of their Genius more inclinable to act than to write; seeing as well they as we have lived unacquainted with these actions of our Nation, until such time as a Foreign Author to our Country came to tell them.

Besides the merits of this Piece for its curiosity, another point of no less esteem, is the truth and sincerity wherewith everything seemeth to be penned. No greater ornament or dignity can be added unto History, either humane or natural, than truth. All other embellishments, if this be failing, are of little or no esteem; if this be delivered, are either needless or superfluous. What concerneth this requisite in our Author, his lines do everywhere declare the faithfulness and sincerity of his mind. He writeth not by hearsay, but was an eye witness, as he somewhere telleth you, unto all and every one of the bold and hazardous attempts which he relateth. And these he delivereth with such candour of stile, such ingenuity of mind, such plainness of words, such conciseness of periods, so much divested of Rhetorical Hyperboles, or the least flourishes of Eloquence, so hugely void of Passion or national Reflections, as that he strongly perswadeth all-along to the credit of what he saith; yea, raiseth the mind of the Reader to believe these things far greater than what he hath said; and having read him, leaveth onely this scruple or concern behind, that you can read him no longer. In a word, such are his deserts, that some persons peradventure would not stickle to compare him to the Father of Historians, Philip de Comines; at least thus much may be said, with all truth imaginable, that he resembleth that great Author in many of his excellent qualities.

I know some persons have objected against the greatness of these prodigious Adventures, intimating that the resistance our Bucaniers found in America, was everywhere but small. For the Spaniards, say they, in the West Indies, are become of late years nothing less, but rather much more degenerate than in Europe. The continual Peace they have enjoyed in those parts, the defect of Military Discipline, and European souldiers for their Commanders, much contributing hereunto. But more especially, and above all other reasons, the very luxury of the Soil and Riches, the extreme heat of those Countries, and influence of the Stars being such, as totally inclineth their bodies unto an infinite effeminacy and cowardize of minds.

Unto these Reasons I shall only answer in brief. This History will convince them to be manifestly false. For as to the continual Peace here alleadged, we know that no Peace could ever be established beyond the Line, since the first possession of the West-Indies by the Spaniards, till the burning of Panama. At that time, or few months before, Sir William Godolphin by his prudent negotiation in quality of Embassadour for our most Gracious Monarch, did conclude at Madrid a peace to be observed even beyond the Line, and through the whole extent of the Spanish Dominions in the West-Indies. This transaction gave the Spaniards new causes of complaints against our proceedings, that no sooner a Peace had been established for those parts of America, but our forces had taken and burnt both Chagre, St. Catherine, and Panama. But our reply was convincing, That whereas eight or ten months of time had been allowed by Articles for the publishing of the said Peace through all the Dominions of both Monarchies in America, those Hostilities had been committed, not onely without orders from his Majesty of England, but also within the space of the said eight or ten months of time. Until that time the Spanish Inhabitants of America being, as it were, in a perpetual War with Europe, certain it is that no Coasts nor Kingdoms in the World have been more frequently infested nor alarm'd with the invasions of several Nations than theirs. Thus from the very beginning of their Conquests in America, both English, French, Dutch Portuguese, Swedes, Danes, Curlanders, and all other nations that navigate the Ocean, have frequented the West-Indies, and filled them with their robberies and Assaults. From these occasions have they been in continual watch and ward, and kept their Militia in constant exercise, as also their Garrisons pretty well provided and paid; as fearing every sail they discovered at Sea, to be Pirats of one Nation or another. But much more especially, since that Curasao, Tortuga, and Jamaica have been inhabited by English, French, and Dutch, and bred up that race of Hunts-men, than which, no other ever was more desperate, nor more mortal enemies to the Spaniards, called Bucaniers. Now shall we say, that these People, through too long continuation of Peace, have utterly abolished the exercises of War, having been all-along incessantly vexed with the Tumults and Alarms thereof?

In like manner is it false, to accuse their defect of Military Discipline for want of European Commanders. For who knoweth not that all places, both Military and Civil, through those vast dominions of the West-Indies, are provided out of Spain? And those of the Militia most commonly given unto expert Commanders, trained up from their infancy in the Wars of Europe, either in Africa, Milan, Sicily, Naples, or Flanders, fighting against either English, French, Dutch, Portuguese, or Moors? Yea their very Garrisons, if you search them in those parts, will peradventure be found to be stock'd three parts to four with Souldiers both born and bred in the Kingdom of Spain.

From these Considerations it may be inferr'd what little difference ought to be allowed betwixt the Spanish Souldiers, Inhabitants of the West-Indies, and those of Europe. And how little the Soil or Climate hath influenced or caused their Courage to degenerate towards cowardize or baseness of mind. As if the very same Argument, deduced from the nature of that Climate, did not equally militate against the valour of our famous Bucaniers, and represent this to be of as degenerate Metal as theirs.

But nothing can be more clearly evinced, than is the Valour of the American Spaniards, either Souldiers or Officers, by the sequel of this History. What men ever fought more desperately than the Garrison of Chagre? Their number being 314, and of all these, only thirty remaining; of which number scarce ten were unwounded; and among them, not one officer found alive? Were not 600 killed upon the spot at Panama, 500 at Gibraltar, almost as many more at Puerto del Principe, all dying with their Arms in their hands, and facing bravely the Enemy for the defence of their Country and private Concerns? Did not those of the Town of San Pedro both fortifie themselves, lay several Ambuscades, and lastly sell their lives as dear as any European Souldier could do; Lolonois being forced to gain step by step his advance unto the Town, with huge loss both of bloud and men? Many other instances might be produced out of this compendious Volume, of the generous resistance the Spaniards made in several places, though Fortune favoured not their Arms.

Next, as to the personal Valour of many of their Commanders, What man ever behaved himself more briskly than the Governour of Gibraltar, than the Governour of Puerto del Principe, both dying for the defence of their Towns; than Don Alonso del Campo, and others? Or what examples can easily parallel the desperate courage of the Governour of Chagre? who, though the Palizda's were fired, the Terraplens were sunk into the Ditch, the Breaches were entred, the Houses all burnt above him, the whole Castle taken, his men all killed; yet would not admit of any quarter, but chose rather to die under his Arms, being shot into the brain, than surrender himself as a Prisoner unto the Bucaniers. What lion ever fought to the last gasp more obstinately than the Governour of Puerto Velo? who, seeing the Town enter'd by surprizal in the night, one chief Castle blown up into the Air, all the other Forts and Castles taken, his own assaulted several ways, both Religious men and women placed at the front of the Enemy to fix the Ladders against the Walls; yet spared not to kill as many of the said Religious persons as he could. And at last, the walls being scaled, the Castle enter'd and taken, all his own men overcome by fire and sword, who had cast down their Arms, and begged mercy from the Enemy; yet would admit of none for his own life. Yet, with his own hands killed several of his Souldiers, to force them to stand to their Arms, though all were lost. Yea, though his own Wife and Daughter begged of him upon their knees that he would have his life by craving quarter, though the Enemy desired of him the same thing; yet would hearken to no cries nor perswasions, but they were forced to kill him, combating with his Arms in his hands, being not otherwise able to take him Prisoner, as they were desirous to do. Shall these men be said to be influenced with Cowardize, who thus acted to the very last Scene of their own Tragedies? Or shall we rather say that they wanted no Courage, but Fortune? It being certainly true, that he who is killed in a Batel, may be equally couragious with him that killeth. And that whosoever derogateth from the Valour of the Spaniards in the West-Indies, diminisheth in like manner the Courage of the Bucaniers, his own Country-men, who have seemed to act beyond mortal men in America.

Now, to say something concerning John Esquemeling, the first Author of this History. I take him to be a Dutch-man, or at least born in Flanders, notwithstanding that the Spanish Translation representeth him to be a Native of the Kingdom of France. His printing this History originally in Dutch, which doubtless must be his native Tongue, who otherwise was but an illiterate man, together with the very sound of his name, convincing me thereunto. True it is, he set sail from France, and was some years at Tortuga; but neither of these two Arguments, drawn from the History, are prevalent. For were he to be a French-man born, how came he to learn the Dutch language so perfectly as to prefer it to his own? Especially that not being spoken at Tortuga nor Jamaica, where he resided all the while.

I hope I have made this English Translation something more plain and correct than the Spanish. Some few notorious faults either of the Printer or the Interpreter, I am sure I have redressed. But the Spanish Translator complaining much of the intricacy of Stile in the Original (as flowing from a person who, as hath been said, was no Scholar) as he was pardonable, being in great haste, for not rendring his own Version so distinct and elaborate as he could desire; so must I be excused from the one, that is to say, Elegancy, if I have cautiously declined the other, I mean Confusion.

The Pirates of Panama - The Buccaneers of America

Chapter I

The introduction—The author sets forth for the Western islands, in the service of the West-India Company of France—They meet with an English frigate, and arrive at the Island of Tortuga.

WE set sail from Havre-de-Grace in France, from whence we set sail in the ship called St. John, May 2, 1666. Our vessel was equipped with twenty-eight guns, twenty mariners, and two hundred and twenty passengers, including those whom the company sent as free passengers. Soon after we came to an anchor under the Cape of Barfleur, there to join seven other ships of the same West-India company, which were to come from Dieppe, under convoy of a man-of-war, mounted with thirty-seven guns, and two hundred and fifty men. Of these ships two were bound for Senegal, five for the Caribbee islands, and ours for Tortuga. Here gathered to us about twenty sail of other ships, bound for Newfoundland, with some Dutch vessels going for Nantz, Rochel, and St. Martin's, so that in all we made thirty sail. Here we put ourselves in a posture of defence, having noticed that four English frigates, of sixty guns each, waited for us near Aldernay. Our admiral, the Chevalier Sourdis, having given necessary orders, we sailed thence with a favourable gale, and some mists arising, totally impeded the English frigates from discovering our fleet. We steered our course as near as we could to the coast of France, for fear of the enemy. As we sailed along, we met a vessel of Ostend, who complained to our admiral, that a French privateer had robbed him that very morning; whereupon we endeavoured to pursue the said pirate; but our labour was in vain, not being able to overtake him.

Our fleet, as we sailed, caused no small fears and alarms to the inhabitants of the coasts of France, these judging us to be English, and that we sought some convenient place for landing. To allay their fright, we hung out our colours; but they would not trust us. After this we came to an anchor in the bay of Conquet in Brittany, near Ushant, there to take in water. Having stored ourselves with fresh provisions here, we prosecuted our voyage, designing to pass by the Ras of Fontenau, and not expose ourselves to the Sorlingues, fearing the English that were cruising thereabouts. The river Ras is of a current very strong and rapid, which, rolling over many rocks, disgorges itself into the sea, on the coast of France, in 48 deg. 10 min. latitude; so that this passage is very dangerous, all the rocks, as yet, being not thoroughly known.

Here I shall mention the ceremony, which, at this passage, and some other places, is used by the mariners, and by them called baptism, though it may seem little to our purpose. The master's mate clothed himself with a ridiculous sort of garment, that reached to his feet, and on his head he put a suitable cap, made very burlesque; in his right hand he had a naked wooden sword, and in his left a pot full of ink: his face was horribly blacked with soot, and his neck adorned with a collar of many little pieces of wood. Thus apparelled, he commanded every one to be called who had never passed through that dangerous place before; and then, causing them to kneel down, he made the sign of the cross on their foreheads, with ink, and gave every one a stroke on the shoulders with his wooden sword. Meanwhile, the standers-by cast a bucket of water upon each man's head; and so ended the ceremony. But that done, each of the baptized must give a bottle of brandy, placing it nigh the main-mast, without speaking a word; even those who have no such liquor not being excused. If the vessel never passed that way before, the captain is obliged to distribute some wine among the mariners and passengers; but as for other gifts, which the newly-baptized frequently offer, they are divided among the old seamen, and of them they make a banquet among themselves.

The Hollanders likewise, not only at this passage, but also at the rocks called Berlingues, nigh the coast of Portugal, in 39 deg. 40 min. (being a passage very dangerous, especially by night, when, in the dark, the rocks are not distinguishable, the land being very high) they use some such ceremony: but their manner of baptizing is very different from that of the French; for he that is to be baptized is fastened, and hoisted up thrice, at the mainyard's end, as if he were a criminal. If he be hoisted the fourth time, in the name of the Prince of Orange, or of the captain of the vessel, his honour is more than ordinary. Thus every one is dipped several times in the main ocean; but he that is dipped first has the honour of being saluted with a gun. Such as are not willing to fall, must pay twelve pence for ransom; if he be an officer, two shillings; and if a passenger, at their own pleasure. If the ship never passed that way before, the captain is to give a small rundlet of wine, which, if he denies, the mariners may cut off the stem of the vessel. All the profit accruing by this ceremony is kept by the master's mate, who, after reaching their port, usually lays it out in wine, which is drank amongst the ancient seamen. Some say this ceremony was instituted by the Emperor Charles V. though it is not amongst his laws. But here I leave these sea customs, and return to our voyage.

Having passed the Ras, we had very good weather, till we came to Cape Finis Terræ: here a sudden tempest surprised us, and separated our ship from the rest that were in our company. This storm continued eight days; in which time it would move compassion to see how miserably the passengers were tumbled to and fro, on all sides of the ship; insomuch, that the mariners, in the performance of their duty, were compelled to tread upon them. This boisterous weather being over, we had very favourable gales again, till we came to the tropic of Cancer. This tropic is an imaginary circle, which astronomers have invented in the heavens, limiting the progress of the sun towards the north pole. It is placed in the latitude of 23 deg. 30 min. Here we were baptized a second time, as before. The French always perform this ceremony at the tropic of Cancer, as also under the tropic of Capricorn. In this part of the world we had very favourable weather, at which we were very glad, because of our great want of water; for that element is so scarce with us, that we were stinted to two half pints a man every day.

About the latitude of Barbadoes, we met an English frigate, or privateer, who first began to give us chase; but finding herself not to exceed us in force, presently got away: hereupon, we pursued her, firing several guns, eight-pounders, at her; but at length she escaped, and we returned to our course. Soon after, we came within sight of Martinico. We were bent to the coast of the isle of St. Peter, but were frustrated by a storm, which took us hereabouts. Hence we resolved to steer to Gaudaloupe, yet we could not reach this island, by reason of the said storm; so that we directed our course to the isle of Tortuga, being the very same land we were bound to. We passed along the coast of Punta Rica, which is extremely agreeable and delightful to the sight, being adorned with beautiful woods, even to the tops of the mountains. Then we discovered Hispaniola (of which I shall give a description), and we coasted about it till we came to Tortuga, our desired port. Here we anchored, July 7, in the same year, not having lost one man in the voyage. We landed the goods that belonged to the West-India company, and, soon after, the ship was sent to Cal de Sac with some passengers.

Chapter II

A description of Tortuga—The fruits and plants there—How the French first settled there, at two several times, and forced out the Spaniards—The author twice sold in the said island.

THE island of Tortuga is situate on the north side of Hispaniola, in 20 deg. 30 min. latitude; its just extent is threescore leagues about. The Spaniards, who gave name to this island, called it so from the shape of the land, in some manner resembling a great sea-tortoise, called by them Tortuga-de-mar. The country is very mountainous, and full of rocks, and yet thick of lofty trees, that grow upon the hardest of those rocks, without partaking of a softer soil. Hence it comes that their roots, for the greatest part, are seen naked, entangled among the rocks like the branching of ivy against our walls. That part of this island which stretches to the north is totally uninhabited: the reason is, first, because it is incommodious, and unhealthy: and, secondly, for the ruggedness of the coast, that gives no access to the shore, unless among rocks almost inaccessible: for this cause it is peopled only on the south part, which hath only one port indifferently good: yet this harbour has two entries, or channels, which afford passage to ships of seventy guns; the port itself being without danger, and capable of receiving a great number of vessels. The inhabited parts, of which the first is called the Low-Lands, or Low-Country: this is the chief among the rest, because it contains the port aforesaid. The town is called Cayona, and here live the chiefest and richest planters of the island. The second part is called the Middle Plantation: its soil is yet almost new, being only known to be good for tobacco. The third is named Ringot, and is situate towards the west part of the island. The fourth and last is called the Mountain, in which place were made the first plantations upon this island.

As to the wood that grows here, we have already said that the trees are exceeding tall, and pleasing to the sight; whence no man will doubt, but they may be applied to several uses. Such is the yellow saunder, which by the inhabitants is called bois de chandel, or, in English, candle-wood, because it burns like a candle, and serves them with light while they fish by night. Here grows, also, lingnum sanctum, or guaiacum: its virtues are very well known, more especially to those who observe not the Seventh Commandment, and are given to impure copulations!—physicians drawing hence, in several compositions, the greatest antidote for venereal diseases; as also for cold and viscous humours. The trees, likewise, which afford gummi elemi, grow here in great abundance; as doth radix Chinæ, or China root: yet this is not so good as that of other parts of the western world. It is very white and soft, and serves for pleasant food to the wild boars, when they can find nothing else. This island, also, is not deficient in aloes, nor an infinite number of the other medicinal herbs, which may please the curiosity of such as are given to their contemplation: moreover, for building of ships, or any other sort of architecture, here are found several sorts of timber. The fruits, likewise, which grow here abundantly, are nothing inferior, in quantity or quality, to what other islands produce. I shall name only some of the most ordinary and common: such are magnoit, potatoes, Abajou apples, yannas, bacones, paquays, carosoles, mamayns, annananes, and divers other sorts, which I omit to specify. Here grow likewise, in great numbers, those trees called palmitoes, or palmites, whence is drawn a certain juice which serves the inhabitants instead of wine, and whose leaves cover their houses instead of tiles.

In this island aboundeth, also, the wild boar. The governor hath prohibited the hunting of them with dogs, fearing lest, the island being but small, the whole race of them, in a short time, should be destroyed. The reason why he thought convenient to preserve these wild beasts was, that, in case of any invasion, the inhabitants might sustain themselves with their food, especially were they once constrained to retire to the woods and mountains. Yet this sort of game is almost impeded by itself, by reason of the many rocks and precipices, which, for the greatest part, are covered with little shrubs, very green and thick; whence the huntsmen have oftentimes fallen, and left us the sad remembrance of many a memorable disaster.

At a certain time of the year there resort to Tortuga large flocks of wild pigeons, and then the inhabitants feed on them very plentifully, having more than they can consume, and leaving totally to their repose all other sorts of fowl, both wild and tame; that so, in the absence of the pigeons, these may supply their place. But as nothing in the universe, though never so pleasant, can be found, but what hath something of bitterness with it; the very symbol of this truth we see in the aforesaid pigeons: for these, the season being past, can scarce be touched with the tongue, they become so extremely lean, and bitter even to admiration. The reason of this bitterness is attributed to a certain seed which they eat about that time, even as bitter as gall. About the sea-shores, everywhere, are found great multitudes of crabs, both of land and sea, and both sorts very big. These are good to feed servants and slaves, whose palates they please, but are very hurtful to the sight: besides, being eaten too often, they cause great giddiness in the head, with much weakness of the brain; so that, very frequently, they are deprived of sight for a quarter of an hour.

The French having settled in the isle of St. Christopher, planted there a sort of trees, of which, at present, there possibly may be greater quantities; with the timber whereof they made long-boats, and hoys, which they sent thence westward, well manned and victualled, to discover other islands. These setting sail from St. Christopher, came within sight of Hispaniola, where they arrived with abundance of joy. Having landed, they marched into the country, where they found large quantities of cattle; such as cows, bulls, horses, and wild boars: but finding no great profit in these animals, unless they could enclose them, and knowing, likewise, the island to be pretty well peopled by the Spaniards, they thought it convenient to enter upon and seize the island of Tortuga. This they performed without any difficulty, there being upon the island no more than ten or twelve Spaniards to guard it.

These few men let the French come in peaceably, and possess the island for six months, without any trouble; meanwhile they passed and repassed, with their canoes, to Hispaniola, from whence they transported many people, and at last began to plant the whole island of Tortuga. The few Spaniards remaining there, perceiving the French to increase their number daily, began, at last, to repine at their prosperity, and grudge them the possession: hence they gave notice to others of their nation, their neighbours, who sent several boats, well armed and manned, to dispossess the French. This expedition succeeded according to their desires; for the new possessors, seeing the great number of Spaniards, fled with all they had to the woods, and hence, by night, they wafted over with canoes to the island of Hispaniola: this they the more easily performed, having no women or children with them, nor any great substance to carry away. Here they also retired into the woods, both to seek for food, and from thence, with secrecy, to give intelligence to others of their own faction; judging for certain, that within a little while they should be in a capacity to hinder the Spaniards from fortifying in Tortuga.

Meanwhile, the Spaniards of the great island ceased not to seek after their new guests, the French, with intent to root them out of the woods if possible, or cause them to perish with hunger; but this design soon failed, having found that the French were masters both of good guns, powder, and bullets. Here therefore the fugitives waited for a certain opportunity, wherein they knew the Spaniards were to come from Tortuga with arms, and a great number of men, to join with those of the greater island for their destruction. When this occasion offered, they in the meanwhile deserting the woods where they were, returned to Tortuga, and dispossessed the small number of Spaniards that remained at home. Having so done, they fortified themselves the best they could, thereby to prevent the return of the Spaniards in case they should attempt it. Moreover, they sent immediately to the governor of St. Christopher's, craving his aid and relief, and demanding of him a governor, the better to be united among themselves, and strengthened on all occasions. The governor of St. Christopher's received their petition with much satisfaction, and, without delay, sent Monsieur le Passeur to them in quality of a governor, together with a ship full of men, and all necessaries for their establishment and defence. No sooner had they received this recruit, but the governor commanded a fortress to be built upon the top of a high rock, from whence he could hinder the entrance of any ships or other vessels to the port. To this fort no other access could be had, than by almost climbing through a very narrow passage that was capable only of receiving two persons at once, and those not without difficulty. In the middle of this rock was a great cavity, which now serves for a storehouse: besides, here was great convenience for raising a battery. The fort being finished, the governor commanded two guns to be mounted, which could not be done without great toil and labour; as also a house to be built within the fort, and afterwards the narrow way, that led to the said fort, to be broken and demolished, leaving no other ascent thereto than by a ladder. Within the fort gushes out a plentiful fountain of pure fresh water, sufficient to refresh a garrison of a thousand men. Being possessed of these conveniences, and the security these things might promise, the French began to people the island, and each of them to seek their living; some by hunting, others by planting tobacco, and others by cruizing and robbing upon the coasts of the Spanish islands, which trade is continued by them to this day.

The Spaniards, notwithstanding, could not behold, but with jealous eyes, the daily increase of the French in Tortuga, fearing lest, in time, they might by them be dispossessed also of Hispaniola. Thus taking an opportunity (when many of the French were abroad at sea, and others employed in hunting), with eight hundred men, in several canoes, they landed again in Tortuga, almost without being perceived by the French; but finding that the governor had cut down many trees for the better discovery of any enemy in case of an assault, as also that nothing of consequence could be done without great guns, they consulted about the fittest place for raising a battery. This place was soon concluded to be the top of a mountain which was in sight, seeing that from thence alone they could level their guns at the fort, which now lay open to them since the cutting down of the trees by the new possessors. Hence they resolved to open a way for the carriage of some pieces of ordnance to the top. This mountain is somewhat high, and the upper part thereof plain, from whence the whole island may be viewed: the sides thereof are very rugged, by reason a great number of inaccessible rocks do surround it; so that the ascent was very difficult, and would always have been the same, had not the Spaniards undergone the immense labour and toil of making the way before mentioned, as I shall now relate.

The Spaniards had with them many slaves and Indians, labouring men, whom they call matades, or, in English, half-yellow men; these they ordered with iron tools to dig a way through the rocks. This they performed with the greatest speed imaginable; and through this way, by the help of many ropes and pulleys, they at last made shift to get up two pieces of ordnance, wherewith they made a battery next day, to play on the fort. Meanwhile, the French knowing these designs, prepared for a defence (while the Spaniards were busy about the battery) sending notice everywhere to their companions for help. Thus the hunters of the island all joined together, and with them all the pirates who were not already too far from home. These landed by night at Tortuga, lest they should be seen by the Spaniards; and, under the same obscurity of the night, they all together, by a back way, climbed the mountain where the Spaniards were posted, which they did the more easily being acquainted with these rocks. They came up at the very instant that the Spaniards, who were above, were preparing to shoot at the fort, not knowing in the least of their coming. Here they set upon them at their backs with such fury as forced the greatest part to precipitate themselves from the top to the bottom, and dash their bodies in pieces: few or none escaped; for if any remained alive, they were put to the sword. Some Spaniards did still keep the bottom of the mountain; but these, hearing the shrieks and cries of them that were killed, and believing some tragical revolution to be above, fled immediately towards the sea, despairing ever to regain the island of Tortuga.

The governors of this island behaved themselves as proprietors and absolute lords thereof till 1664, when the West-India company of France took possession thereof, and sent thither, for their governor, Monsieur Ogeron. These planted the colony for themselves by their factors and servants, thinking to drive some considerable trade from thence with the Spaniards, even as the Hollanders do from Curacao: but this design did not answer; for with other nations they could drive no trade, by reason they could not establish any secure commerce from the beginning with their own; forasmuch as at the first institution of this company in France they agreed with the pirates, hunters, and planters, first possessors of Tortuga, that these should buy all their necessaries from the said company upon trust. And though this agreement was put in execution, yet the factors of the company soon after found that they could not recover either monies or returns from those people, that they were constrained to bring some armed men into the island, in behalf of the company, to get in some of their payments. But neither this endeavour, nor any other, could prevail towards the settling a second trade with those of the island. Hereupon, the company recalled their factors, giving them orders to sell all that was their own in the said plantation, both the servants belonging to the company (which were sold, some for twenty, and others for thirty pieces of eight), as also all other merchandizes and proprieties. And thus all their designs fell to the ground.

On this occasion I was also sold, being a servant under the said company in whose service I left France: but my fortune was very bad, for I fell into the hands of the most cruel and perfidious man that ever was born, who was then governor, or rather lieutenant-general, of that island. This man treated me with all the hard usage imaginable, yea, with that of hunger, with which I thought I should have perished inevitably. Withal, he was willing to let me buy my freedom and liberty, but not under the rate of three hundred pieces of eight, I not being master of one at a time in the world. At last, through the manifold miseries I endured, as also affliction of mind, I was thrown into a dangerous sickness. This misfortune, added to the rest, was the cause of my happiness: for my wicked master, seeing my condition, began to fear lest he should lose his monies with my life. Hereupon he sold me a second time to a surgeon, for seventy pieces of eight. Being with this second master, I began soon to recover my health through the good usage I received, he being much more humane and civil than my first patron. He gave me both clothes and very good food; and after I had served him but one year, he offered me my liberty, with only this condition, that I should pay him one hundred pieces of eight when I was in a capacity so to do; which kind proposal of his I could not but accept with infinite joy and gratitude.

Being now at liberty, though like Adam when he was first created—that is, naked and destitute of all human necessaries—not knowing how to get my living, I determined to enter into the order of the pirates or robbers at sea. Into this society I was received with common consent, both of the superior and vulgar sort, where I continued till 1672. Having assisted them in all their designs and attempts, and served them in many notable exploits (of which hereafter I shall give the reader a true account), I returned to my own native country. But before I begin my relation, I shall say something of the island Hispaniola, which lies towards the western part of America; as also give my reader a brief description thereof, according to my slender ability and experience.

Chapter III

A Description of Hispaniola.—Also a Relation of the French Buccaneers.

THE large and rich island called Hispaniola is situate from 17 degrees to 19 degrees latitude; the circumference is 300 leagues; the extent from east to west 120; its breadth almost 50, being broader or narrower at certain places. This island was first discovered by Christopher Columbus, a.d. 1492; he being sent for this purpose by Ferdinand, king of Spain; from which time to this present the Spaniards have been continually possessors thereof. There are upon this island very good and strong cities, towns, and hamlets, as well as a great number of pleasant country houses and plantations, the effects of the care and industry of the Spaniards its inhabitants.

The chief city and metropolis hereof is Santo Domingo; being dedicated to St. Dominic, from whom it derives its name. It is situate towards the south, and affords a most excellent prospect; the country round about being embellished with innumerable rich plantations, as also verdant meadows and fruitful gardens; all which produce plenty and variety of excellent pleasant fruits, according to the nature of those countries. The governor of the island resides in this city, which is, as it were, the storehouse of all the cities, towns, and villages, which hence export and provide themselves with all necessaries for human life; and yet hath it this particularity above many other cities, that it entertains no commerce with any nation but its own, the Spaniards. The greatest part of the inhabitants are rich and substantial merchants or shopkeepers.

Another city of this island is San Jago, or St. James, being consecrated to that apostle. This is an open place, without walls or castle, situate in 19 deg. latitude. The inhabitants are generally hunters and planters, the adjacent territory and soil being very proper for the said exercises: the city is surrounded with large and delicious fields, as much pleasing to the view as those of Santo Domingo; and these abound with beasts both wild and tame, yielding vast numbers of skins and hides, very profitable to the owners.

In the south part of this island is another city, called Nuestra Sennora de Alta Gracia. This territory produces great quantities of cacao, whereof the inhabitants make great store of the richest chocolate. Here grows also ginger and tobacco, and much tallow is made of the beasts which are hereabouts hunted.

The inhabitants of this beautiful island of Hispaniola often resort in their canoes to the isle of Savona, not far distant, where is their chief fishery, especially of tortoises. Hither those fish constantly resort in great multitudes, at certain seasons, there to lay their eggs, burying them in the sands of the shoal, where, by the heat of the sun, which in those parts is very ardent, they are hatched. This island of Savona has little or nothing that is worthy consideration, being so very barren by reason of its sandy soil. True it is, that here grows some small quantity of lignum sanctum, or guaiacum, of whose use we say something in another place.

Westward of Santo Domingo is another great village called El Pueblo de Aso, or the town of Aso: the inhabitants thereof drive great traffic with those of another village, in the very middle of the island, and is called San Juan de Goave, or St. John of Goave. This is environed with a magnificent prospect of gardens, woods, and meadows. Its territory extends above twenty leagues in length, and grazes a great number of wild bulls and cows. In this village scarce dwell any others than hunters and butchers, who flay the beasts that are killed. These are for the most part a mongrel sort of people; some of which are born of white European people and negroes, and called mulattoes: others of Indians and white people, and termed mesticos: but others come of negroes and Indians, and are called alcatraces. From the said village are exported yearly vast quantities of tallow and hides, they exercising no other traffic: for as to the lands in this place, they are not cultivated, by reason of the excessive dryness of the soil. These are the chiefest places that the Spaniards possess in this island, from the Cape of Lobos towards St. John de

Goave, unto the Cape of Samana nigh the sea, on the north side, and from the eastern part towards the sea, called Punta de Espada. All the rest of the island is possessed by the French, who are also planters and hunters.

This island hath very good ports for ships, from the Cape of Lobos to the Cape of Tiburon, on the west side thereof. In this space there are no less than four ports, exceeding in goodness, largeness, and security, even the very best of England. Besides these, from the Cape of Tiburon to the Cape of Donna Maria, there are two very excellent ports; and from this cape to the Cape of St. Nicholas, there are no less than twelve others. Every one of these ports hath also the confluence of two or three good rivers, in which are great plenty of several sorts of fish very pleasing to the palate. The country hereabouts is well watered with large and deep rivers and brooks, so that this part of the land may easily be cultivated without any great fear of droughts, because of these excellent streams. The sea-coasts and shores are also very pleasant, to which the tortoises resort in large numbers to lay their eggs.

This island was formerly very well peopled, on the north side, with many towns and villages; but these, being ruined by the Hollanders, were at last, for the greatest part, deserted by the Spaniards.

The spacious fields of this island commonly are five or six leagues in length, the beauty whereof is so pleasing to the eye, that, together with the great variety of their natural productions, they captivate the senses of the beholder. For here at once they not only with diversity of objects recreate the sight, but with many of the same do also please the smell, and with most contribute delights to the taste; also they flatter and excite the appetite, especially with the multitudes of oranges and lemons here growing, both sweet and sour, and those that participate of both tastes, and are only pleasantly tartish. Besides here abundantly grow several sorts of fruit, such are citrons, toronjas, and limas; in English not improperly called crab lemons.

Beside the fruit which this island produces, whose plenty, as is said, surpasses all the islands of America; it abounds also with all sorts of quadrupeds, as horses, bulls, cows, wild boars, and others, very useful to mankind, not only for food, but for cultivating the ground, and the management of commerce.

Here are vast numbers of wild dogs: these destroy yearly many cattle; for no sooner hath a cow calved, or a mare foaled, but these wild mastiffs devour the young, if they find not resistance from keepers and domestic dogs. They run up and down the woods and fields, commonly fifty, threescore, or more, together; being withal so fierce, that they will often assault an entire herd of wild boars, not ceasing to worry them till they have fetched down two or three. One day a French buccaneer showed me a strange action of this kind: being in the fields a-hunting together, we heard a great noise of dogs which has surrounded a wild boar: having tame dogs with us, we left them to the custody of our servants, being desirous to see the sport. Hence my companion and I climbed up two several trees, both for security and prospect. The wild boar, all alone, stood against a tree, defending himself with his tusks from a great number of dogs that enclosed him; killed with his teeth, and wounded several of them. This bloody fight continued about an hour; the wild boar, meanwhile, attempting many times to escape. At last flying, one dog, leaping upon his back, fastened on his throat. The rest of the dogs, perceiving the courage of their companion, fastened likewise on the boar, and presently killed him. This done, all of them, the first only excepted, laid themselves down upon the ground about the prey, and there peaceably continued, till he, the first and most courageous of the troop, had ate as much as he could: when this dog had left off, all the rest fell in to take their share, till nothing was left. What ought we to infer from this notable action, performed by wild animals, but this: that even beasts themselves are not destitute of knowledge, and that they give us documents how to honour such as have deserved well; even since these irrational animals did reverence and respect him that exposed his life to the greatest danger against the common enemy?

The governor of Tortuga, Monsieur Ogeron, finding that the wild dogs killed so many of the wild boars, that the hunters of that island had much ado to find any; fearing lest that common substance of the island should fail, sent for a great quantity of poison from France to destroy the wild mastiffs: this was done, a.d. 1668, by commanding horses to be killed, and empoisoned, and laid open at certain places where the wild dogs used to resort. This being continued for six months, there were killed an incredible number; and yet all this could not exterminate and destroy the race, or scarce diminish them; their number appearing almost as large as before. These wild dogs are easily tamed among men, even as tame as ordinary house dogs. The hunters of those parts, whenever they find a wild bitch with whelps, commonly take away the puppies, and bring them home; which being grown up, they hunt much better than other dogs.

But here the curious reader may perhaps inquire how so many wild dogs came here. The occasion was, the Spaniards having possessed these isles, found them peopled with Indians, a barbarous people, sensual and brutish, hating all labour, and only inclined to killing, and making war against their neighbours; not out of ambition, but only because they agreed not with themselves in some common terms of language; and perceiving the dominion of the Spaniards laid great restrictions upon their lazy and brutish customs, they conceived an irreconcilable hatred against them; but especially because they saw them take possession of their kingdoms and dominions. Hereupon, they made against them all the resistance they could, opposing everywhere their designs to the utmost: and the Spaniards finding themselves cruelly hated by the Indians, and nowhere secure from their treacheries, resolved to extirpate and ruin them, since they could neither tame them by civility, nor conquer them with the sword. But the Indians, it being their custom to make the woods their chief places of defence, at present made these their refuge, whenever they fled from the Spaniards. Hereupon, those first conquerors of the New World made use of dogs to range and search the intricatest thickets of woods and forests for those their implacable and unconquerable enemies: thus they forced them to leave their old refuge, and submit to the sword, seeing no milder usage would do it; hereupon they killed some of them, and quartering their bodies, placed them in the highways, that others might take warning from such a punishment; but this severity proved of ill consequence, for instead of fighting them and reducing them to civility, they conceived such horror of the Spaniards, that they resolved to detest and fly their sight for ever; hence the greatest part died in caves and subterraneous places of the woods and mountains, in which places I myself have often seen great numbers of human bones. The Spaniards finding no more Indians to appear about the woods, turned away a great number of dogs they had in their houses, and they finding no masters to keep them, betook themselves to the woods and fields to hunt for food to preserve their lives; thus by degrees they became unacquainted with houses, and grew wild. This is the truest account I can give of the multitudes of wild dogs in these parts.

But besides these wild mastiffs, here are also great numbers of wild horses everywhere all over the island: they are but low of stature, short bodied, with great heads, long necks, and big or thick legs: in a word, they have nothing handsome in their shape. They run up and down commonly in troops of two or three hundred together, one going always before to lead the multitude: when they meet any person travelling through the woods or fields, they stand still, suffering him to approach till he can almost touch them: and then suddenly starting, they betake themselves to flight, running away as fast as they can. The hunters catch them only for their skins, though sometimes they preserve their flesh likewise, which they harden with smoke, using it for provisions when they go to sea.

Here would be also wild bulls and cows in great number, if by continual hunting they were not much diminished; yet considerable profit is made to this day by such as make it their business to kill them. The wild bulls are of a vast bigness of body, and yet they hurt not any one except they be exasperated. Their hides are from eleven to thirteen feet long.

It is now time to speak of the French who inhabit great part of this island. We have already told how they came first into these parts: we shall now only describe their manner of living, customs, and ordinary employments. The callings or professions they follow are generally but three, either to hunt or plant, or else to rove the seas as pirates. It is a constant custom among them all, to seek out a comrade or companion, whom we may call partner in their fortunes, with whom they join the whole stock of what they possess towards a common gain. This is done by articles agreed to, and reciprocally signed. Some constitute their surviving companion absolute heir to what is left by the death of the first: others, if they be married, leave their estates to their wives and children; others, to other relations. This done, every one applies himself to his calling, which is always one of the three afore-mentioned.

The hunters are again subdivided into two sorts; for some of these only hunt wild bulls and cows, others only wild boars. The first of these are called bucaniers, and not long ago were about six hundred on this island, but now they are reckoned about three hundred. The cause has been the great decrease of wild cattle, which has been such, that, far from getting, they now are but poor in their trade. When the bucaniers go into the woods to hunt for wild bulls and cows, they commonly remain there a twelvemonth or two years, without returning home. After the hunt is over, and the spoil divided, they commonly sail to Tortuga, to provide themselves with guns, powder, and shot, and other necessaries for another expedition; the rest of their gains they spend prodigally, giving themselves to all manner of vices and debauchery, particularly to drunkenness, which they practise mostly with brandy: this they drink as liberally as the Spaniards do water. Sometimes they buy together a pipe of wine; this they stave at one end, and never cease drinking till it is out. Thus sottishly they live till they have no money left. The said bucaniers are very cruel and tyrannical to their servants, so that commonly they had rather be galley-slaves, or saw Brazil wood in the rasphouses of Holland, than serve such barbarous masters.

The second sort hunt nothing but wild boars; the flesh of these they salt, and sell it so to the planters. These hunters have the same vicious customs, and are as much addicted to debauchery as the former; but their manner of hunting is different from that in Europe; for these bucaniers have certain places designed for hunting, where they live for three or four months, and sometimes a whole year. Such places are called deza boulan; and in these, with only the company of five or six friends, they continue all the said time in mutual friendship. The first bucaniers many times agree with planters to furnish them with meat all the year at a certain price: the payment hereof is often made with two or three hundredweight of tobacco in the leaf; but the planters commonly into the bargain furnish them with a servant, whom they send to help. To the servant they afford sufficient necessaries for the purpose, especially of powder and shot to hunt withal.

The planters here have but very few slaves; for want of which, themselves and their servants are constrained to do all the drudgery. These servants commonly bind themselves to their masters for three years; but their masters, having no consciences, often traffic with their bodies, as with horses at a fair, selling them to other masters as they sell negroes. Yea, to advance this trade, some persons go purposely into France (and likewise to England, and other countries) to pick up young men or boys, whom they inveigle and transport; and having once got them into these islands, they work them like horses, the toil imposed on them being much harder than what they enjoin the negroes, their slaves; for these they endeavour to preserve, being their perpetual bondmen: but for their white servants, they care not whether they live or die, seeing they are to serve them no longer than three years. These miserable kidnapped people are frequently subject to a disease, which in these parts is called coma, being a total privation of their senses. This distemper is judged to proceed from their hard usage, and the change of their native climate; and there being often among these some of good quality, tender education, and soft constitutions, they are more easily seized with this disease, and others of those countries, than those of harder bodies, and laborious lives. Beside the hard usage in their diet, apparel, and rest, many times they beat them so cruelly, that they fall down dead under the hands of their cruel masters. This I have often seen with great grief. Of the many instances, I shall only give you the following history, it being remarkable in its circumstances.

A certain planter of these countries exercised such cruelty towards one of his servants, as caused him to run away. Having absconded, for some days, in the woods, at last he was taken, and brought back to the wicked Pharaoh. No sooner had he got him, but he commanded him to be tied to a tree; here he gave him so many lashes on his naked back, as made his body run with an entire stream of blood; then, to make the smart of his wounds the greater, he anointed him with lemon-juice, mixed with salt and pepper. In this miserable posture he left him tied to the tree for twenty-four hours, which being past, he began his punishment again, lashing him, as before, so cruelly, that the miserable wretch gave up the ghost, with these dying words: "I beseech the Almighty God, creator of heaven and earth, that he permit the wicked spirit to make thee feel as many torments before thy death, as thou hast caused me to feel before mine." A strange thing, and worthy of astonishment and admiration! Scarce three or four days were past, after this horrible fact, when the Almighty Judge, who had heard the cries of the tormented wretch, suffered the evil one suddenly to possess this barbarous and inhuman homicide, so that those cruel hands which had punished to

27

death his innocent servant, were the tormentors of his own body: for he beat himself and tore his flesh, after a miserable manner, till he lost the very shape of a man; not ceasing to howl and cry, without any rest by day or night. Thus he continued raving mad, till he died. Many other examples of this kind I could rehearse; but these not belonging to our present discourse, I omit them.

The planters of the Caribbee islands are rather worse, and more cruel to their servants, than the former. In the isle of St. Christopher dwells one named Bettesa, well known to the Dutch merchants, who has killed above a hundred of his servants with blows and stripes. The English do the same with their servants; and the mildest cruelty they exercise towards them is, that when they have served six years of their time (they being bound among the English for seven) they use them so cruelly, as to force them to beg of their masters to sell them to others, though it be to begin another servitude of seven years, or at least three or four. And I have known many, who have thus served fifteen or twenty years, before they could obtain their freedom. Another law, very rigorous in that nation, is, if any man owes another above twenty-five shillings English, if he cannot pay it, he is liable to be sold for six or eight months. Not to trouble the reader any longer with relations of this kind, I shall now describe the famous actions and exploits of the greatest pirates of my time, during my residence in those parts: these I shall relate without the least passion or partiality, and assure my reader that I shall give him no stories upon trust, or hearsay, but only those enterprises to which I was myself an eye-witness.

Chapter IV

Original of the most famous pirates of the coasts of America—Famous exploit of Pierre le Grand.

I HAVE told you in the preceding chapters how I was compelled to adventure my life among the pirates of America; which sort of men I name so, because they are not authorized by any sovereign prince: for the kings of Spain having on several occasions sent their ambassadors to the kings of England and France, to complain of the molestations and troubles those pirates often caused on the coasts of America, even in the calm of peace; it hath always been answered, "that such men did not commit those acts of hostility and piracy as subjects to their majesties; and therefore his Catholic Majesty might proceed against them as he should think fit." The king of France added, "that he had no fortress nor castle upon Hispaniola, neither did he receive a farthing of tribute from thence." And the king of England adjoined, "that he had never given any commissions to those of Jamaica, to commit hostilities against the subjects of his Catholic Majesty." Nor did he only give this bare answer, but out of his royal desire to pleasure the court of Spain, recalled the governor of Jamaica, placing another in his room; all which could not prevent these pirates from acting as heretofore. But before I relate their bold actions, I shall say something of their rise and exercises; as also of the chiefest of them, and their manner of arming themselves before they put to sea.

The first pirate that was known upon Tortuga was Pierre le Grand, or Peter the Great. He was born at Dieppe in Normandy. That action which rendered him famous was his taking the vice-admiral of the Spanish flota, near the Cape of Tiburon, on the west side of Hispaniola; this he performed with only one boat, and twenty-eight men. Now till that time the Spaniards had passed and repassed with all security, through the channel of Bahama; so that Pierre le Grand setting out to sea by the Caycos, he took this great ship with all the ease imaginable. The Spaniards they found aboard they set ashore, and sent the vessel to France. The manner how this undaunted spirit attempted and took this large ship I shall give you, out of the journal of the author, in his own words. "The boat," says he, "wherein Pierre le Grand was with his companions, had been at sea a long time without finding any prize worth his taking; and their provisions beginning to fail, they were in danger of starving. Being almost reduced to despair, they spied a great ship of the Spanish flota, separated from the rest; this vessel they resolved to take, or die in the attempt. Hereupon, they sailed towards her, to view her strength. And though they judged the vessel to be superior to theirs, yet their covetousness, and the extremity they were reduced to, made them venture. Being come so near that they could not possibly escape, they made an oath to their captain, Pierre le Grand, to stand by him to the last. 'Tis true, the pirates did believe they should find the ship unprovided to fight, and thereby the sooner master her. It was in the dusk of the evening they began to attack; but before they engaged, they ordered the surgeon of the boat to bore a hole in the sides of it, that their own vessel sinking under them, they might be compelled to attack more vigorously, and endeavour more hastily to board the ship. This was done accordingly, and without any other arms than a pistol in one hand and a sword in the other, they immediately climbed up the sides of the ship, and ran altogether into the great cabin, where they found the captain, with several of his companions, playing at cards. Here they set a pistol to his breast, commanding him to deliver up the ship. The Spaniards, surprised to see the pirates on board their ship, cried 'Jesus bless us! are these devils, or what are they?' Meanwhile some of them took possession of the gun-room, and seized the arms, killing as many as made any opposition; whereupon the Spaniards presently surrendered. That very day the captain of the ship had been told by some of the seamen that the boat which was in view, cruising, was a boat of pirates; whom the captain slightly answered, 'What then, must I be afraid of such a pitiful thing as that is? No, though she were a ship as big and as strong as mine is.' As soon as Pierre le Grand had taken this rich prize, he detained in his service as many of the common seamen as he had need of, setting the rest ashore, and then set sail for France, where he continued, without ever returning to America again."

The planters and hunters of Tortuga had no sooner heard of the rich prize those pirates had taken, but they resolved to follow their example. Hereupon, many of them left their employments, and endeavoured to get some small boats, wherein to exercise piracy; but not being able to purchase, or build them at Tortuga, they resolved to set forth in their canoes, and seek them elsewhere. With these they cruised at first upon Cape de Alvarez, where the Spaniards used to trade from one city to another in small vessels, in which they carry hides, tobacco, and other commodities, to the Havannah, and to which the Spaniards from Europe do frequently resort.

Here it was that those pirates at first took a great many boats laden with the aforesaid commodities; these they used to carry to Tortuga, and sell the whole purchase to the ships that waited for their return, or accidentally happened to be there. With the gains of these prizes they provided themselves with necessaries, wherewith to undertake other voyages, some of which were made to Campechy, and others toward New Spain; in both which the Spaniards then drove a great trade. Upon those coasts they found great numbers of trading vessels, and often ships of great burden. Two of the biggest of these vessels, and two great ships which the Spaniards had laden with plate in the port of Campechy, to go to the Caraccas, they took in less than a month's time, and carried to Tortuga; where the people of the whole island, encouraged by their success, especially seeing in two years the riches of the country so much increased, they augmented the number of pirates so fast, that in a little time there were, in that small island and port, above twenty ships of this sort of people. Hereupon the Spaniards, not able to bear their robberies any longer, equipped two large men-of-war, both for the defence of their own coasts, and to cruise upon the enemies.

Chapter V

How the pirates arm their vessels, and regulate their voyages.

BEFORE the pirates go to sea, they give notice to all concerned, of the day on which they are to embark; obliging each man to bring so many pounds of powder and ball as they think necessary. Being all come aboard, they consider where to get provisions, especially flesh, seeing they scarce eat anything else, and of this the most common sort is pork; the next food is tortoises, which they salt a little: sometimes they rob such or such hog yards, where the Spaniards often have a thousand head of swine together. They come to these places in the night, and having beset the keeper's lodge, they force him to rise, and give them as many heads as they desire, threatening to kill him if he refuses, or makes any noise; and these menaces are oftentimes executed on the miserable swine-keepers, or any other person that endeavours to hinder their robberies.

Having got flesh sufficient for their voyage, they return to their ship: here they allow, twice a day, every one as much as he can eat, without weight or measure; nor does the steward of the vessel give any more flesh, or anything else, to the captain, than to the meanest mariner. The ship being well victualled, they deliberate whither they shall go to seek their desperate fortunes, and likewise agree upon certain articles, which are put in writing, which every one is bound to observe; and all of them, or the chiefest part, do set their hands to it. Here they set down distinctly what sums of money each particular person ought to have for that voyage, the fund of all the payments being what is gotten by the whole expedition; for otherwise it is the same law among these people as with other pirates. No prey, no pay. First, therefore, they mention how much the captain is to have for his ship; next, the salary of the carpenter, or shipwright, who careened, mended, and rigged the vessel: this commonly amounts to one hundred or one hundred and fifty pieces of eight, according to the agreement. Afterwards, for provisions and victualling, they draw out of the same common stock about two hundred pieces of eight; also a salary for the surgeon, and his chest of medicaments, which usually is rated at two hundred or two hundred and fifty pieces of eight. Lastly, they agree what rate each one ought to have that is either wounded or maimed in his body, suffering the loss of any limb; as, for the loss of a right arm, six hundred pieces of eight, or six slaves; for the left arm, five hundred pieces of eight, or five slaves; for a right leg, five hundred pieces of eight, or five slaves; for the left leg, four hundred pieces of eight, or four slaves; for an eye, one hundred pieces of eight, or one slave; for a finger, the same as for an eye. All which sums are taken out of the common stock of what is gotten by their piracy, and a very exact and equal dividend is made of the remainder. They have also regard to qualities and places: thus the captain, or chief, is allotted five or six portions, to what the ordinary seamen have: the master's mate only two, and other officers proportionately to their employ: after which, they draw equal parts from the highest to the lowest mariner, the boys not being omitted, who draw half a share; because when they take a better vessel than their own, it is in the boys' duty to fire their former vessel, and then retire to the prize.

They observe among themselves very good orders; for in the prizes which they take, it is severely prohibited, to every one, to take anything to themselves: hence all they take is equally divided, as hath been said before: yea, they take a solemn oath to each other, not to conceal the least thing they find among the prizes; and if any one is found false to the said oath, he is immediately turned out of the society. They are very civil and charitable to each other; so that if any one wants what another has, with great willingness they give it one to another. As soon as these pirates have taken a prize, they immediately set ashore the prisoners, detaining only some few, for their own help and service: whom, also, they release, after two or three years. They refresh themselves at one island or another, but especially at those on the south of Cuba; here they careen their vessels, while some hunt, and others cruise in canoes for prizes.

The inhabitants of New Spain and Campechy lade their best merchandize in ships of great bulk: the vessels from Campechy sail in the winter to Caraccas, Trinity isles, and that of Margarita, and return back again in the summer. The pirates knowing these seasons (being very diligent in their inquiries) always cruise between the places above-mentioned; but in case they light on no considerable booty, they commonly undertake some more hazardous enterprises: one remarkable instance of which I shall here give you.

A certain pirate called Pierre François, or Peter Francis, waiting a long time at sea with his boat and twenty-six men, for the ships that were to return from Maracaibo to Campechy, and not being able to find any prey, at last he resolved to direct his course to Rancheiras, near the River de la Plata, in 12 deg. and a half north latitude. Here lies a rich bank of pearl, to the fishery whereof they yearly sent from Carthagena twelve vessels with a man-of-war for their defence. Every vessel has at least two negroes in it, who are very dextrous in diving to the depth of six fathoms, where they find good store of pearls. On this fleet, called the pearl-fleet, Pierre François resolved to venture, rather than go home empty; they then rid at anchor at the mouth of the River de la Hacha, the man-of-war scarce half a league distant from the small ships, and the wind very calm. Having spied them in this posture, he presently pulled down his sails, and rowed along the coast feigning to be a Spanish vessel coming from Maracaibo; but no sooner was he come to the pearl-bank, when suddenly he assaulted the vice-admiral of eight guns and sixty men, commanding them to surrender. The Spaniards made a good defence for some time, but at last were forced to submit.

Having thus taken the vice-admiral, he resolved to attempt the man-of-war, with which addition he hoped to master the rest of the fleet: to this end he presently sunk his own boat, putting forth the Spanish colours, and weighed anchor with a little wind which then began to stir, having with threats and promises compelled most of the Spaniards to assist him: but so soon as the man-of-war perceived one of his fleet to sail, he did so too, fearing lest the mariners designed to run away with the riches they had on board. The pirate on this immediately gave over the enterprise, thinking themselves unable to encounter force to force: hereupon they endeavoured to get out of the river and gain the open seas, by making as much sail as they could; which the man-of-war perceiving, he presently gave them chase, but the pirates having laid on too much sail, and a gust of wind suddenly rising, their main-mast was brought by the board, which disabled them from escaping.

This unhappy event much encouraged those in the man-of-war, they gaining upon the pirates every moment, and at last overtook them; but finding they had twenty-two sound men, the rest being either killed or wounded, resolved to defend themselves as long as possible; this they performed very courageously for some time, till they were forced by the man-of-war, on condition that they should not be used as slaves to carry stones, or be employed in other labours for three or four years, as they served their negroes, but that they should be set safe ashore on free land. On these articles they yielded with all they had taken, which was worth, in pearls alone, above 100,000 pieces of eight, besides the vessel, provisions, goods, &c. All of which would have made this a greater prize than he could desire, which he had certainly carried off, if his main-mast had not been lost, as we said before.

Another bold attempt like this, no less remarkable, I shall also give you. A certain pirate of Portugal, thence called Bartholomew Portugues, was cruising in a boat of thirty men and four small guns from Jamaica, upon the Cape de Corriente in Cuba, where he met a great ship from Maracaibo and Carthagena, bound for the Havannah, well provided with twenty great guns and seventy men, passengers and mariners; this ship he presently assaulted, which they on board as resolutely defended. The pirate escaping the first encounter, resolved to attack her more vigorously than before, seeing he had yet suffered no great damage: this he performed with so much resolution, that at last, after a long and dangerous fight, he became master of it. The Portuguese lost only ten men, and had four wounded; so that he had still remaining twenty fighting men, whereas the Spaniards had double the number. Having possessed themselves of the ship, the wind being contrary to return to Jamaica, they resolved to steer to Cape St. Anthony (which lies west of Cuba), there to repair and take in fresh water, of which they were then in great want.

Being very near the cape abovesaid, they unexpectedly met with three great ships coming from New Spain, and bound for the Havannah; by these not being able to escape, they were easily retaken, both ship and pirates, and all made prisoners, and stripped of all the riches they had taken but just before. The cargo consisted in 120,000 weight of cocoa-nuts, the chief ingredient of chocolate, and 70,000 pieces of eight. Two days after this misfortune, there arose a great storm, which separated the ships from one another. The great vessel, where the pirates were, arrived at Campechy, where many considerable merchants came and saluted the captain; these presently knew the Portuguese pirate, being infamous for the many insolencies, robberies and murders he had committed on their coasts, which they kept fresh in their memory.

The next day after their arrival, the magistrates of the city sent to demand the prisoners from on board the ship, in order to punish them according to their deserts; but fearing the captain of the pirates should make his escape (as he had formerly done, being their prisoner once before) they judged it safer to leave him guarded on ship-board for the present, while they erected a gibbet to hang him on the next day, without any other process than to lead him from the ship to his punishment; the rumour of which was presently brought to Bartholomew Portugues, whereby he sought all possible means to escape that night: with this design he took two earthen jars, wherein the Spaniards carry wine from Spain to the West Indies, and stopped them very well, intending to use them for swimming, as those unskilled in that art do corks or empty bladders; having made this necessary preparation, he waited when all should be asleep; but not being able to escape his sentinel's vigilance, he stabbed him with a knife he had secretly purchased, and then threw himself into the sea with the earthen jars before-mentioned, by the help of which, though he never learned to swim, he reached the shore, and immediately took to the woods, where he hid himself for three days, not daring to appear, eating no other food than wild herbs.

Those of the city next day made diligent search for him in the woods, where they concluded him to be. This strict inquiry Portugues saw from the hollow of a tree, wherein he lay hid; and upon their return he made the best of his way to del Golpho Triste, forty leagues from Campechy, where he arrived within a fortnight after his escape: during which time, as also afterwards, he endured extreme hunger and thirst, having no other provision with him than a small calabaca with a little water: besides the fears of falling again into the hands of the Spaniards. He eat nothing but a few shell-fish, which he found among the rocks near the seashore; and being obliged to pass some rivers, not knowing well how to swim, he found at last an old board which the waves had driven ashore, wherein were a few great nails; these he took, and with no small labour whetted on a stone, till he had made them like knives, though not so well; with these, and nothing else, he cut down some branches of trees, which with twigs and osiers he joined together, and made as well as he could a boat to waft him over the rivers: thus arriving at the Cape of

Golpho Triste, as was said, he found a vessel of pirates, comrades of his own, lately come from Jamaica.

To these he related all his adversities and misfortunes, and withal desired they would fit him with a boat and twenty men, with which company alone he promised to return to Campechy, and assault the ship that was in the river, by which he had been taken fourteen days before. They presently granted his request, and equipped him a boat accordingly. With this small company he set out to execute his design, which he bravely performed eight days after he left Golpho Triste; for being arrived at Campechy, with an undaunted courage, and without any noise, he assaulted the said ship: those on board thought it was a boat from land that came to bring contraband goods, and so were in no posture of defence; which opportunity the pirates laying hold of, assaulted them so resolutely, that in a little time they compelled the Spaniards to surrender.

Being masters of the ship, they immediately weighed anchor and set sail from the port, lest they should be pursued by other vessels. This they did with the utmost joy, seeing themselves possessors of so brave a ship; especially Portugues, who by a second turn of fortune was become rich and powerful again, who was so lately in that same vessel a prisoner, condemned to be hanged. With this purchase he designed greater things, which he might have done, since there remained in the vessel so great a quantity of rich merchandise, though the plate had been sent to the city: but while he was making his voyage to Jamaica, near the isle of Pinos, on the south of Cuba, a terrible storm arose, which drove against the Jardines rocks, where she was lost; but Portugues, with his companions, escaped in a canoe, in which he arrived at Jamaica, where it was not long ere he went on new adventures, but was never fortunate after.

Nor less considerable are the actions of another pirate who now lives at Jamaica, who on several occasions has performed very surprising things. He was born at Groninghen in the United Provinces. His own name not being known, his companions gave him that of Roche Brasiliano, by reason of his long residence in Brasil: hence he was forced to fly, when the Portuguese retook those countries from the Dutch, several nations then inhabiting at Brasil (as English, French, Dutch, and others), being constrained to seek new fortunes.

This person fled to Jamaica, where, being at a stand how to get his living, he entered himself into the society of pirates, where he served as a private mariner for some time, and behaved himself so well, that he was beloved and respected by all. One day some of the mariners quarrelled with their captain to that degree, that they left the boat. Brasiliano following them, was chosen their leader, who having fitted out a small vessel, they made him captain.

Within a few days after, he took a great ship coming from New Spain, which had a great quantity of plate on board, and carried it to Jamaica. This action got him a great reputation at home; and though in his private affairs he governed himself very well, he would oftentimes appear brutish and foolish when in drink, running up and down the streets, beating and wounding those he met, no person daring to make any resistance.

To the Spaniards he was always very barbarous and cruel, out of an inveterate hatred against that nation. Of these he commanded several to be roasted alive on wooden spits, for not showing him hog-yards where he might steal swine. After many of these cruelties, as he was cruising on the coasts of Campechy, a dismal tempest surprised him so violently, that his ship was wrecked upon the coasts, the mariners only escaping with their muskets and some few bullets and powder, which were the only things they could save. The ship was lost between Campechy and the Golpho Triste: here they got ashore in a canoe, and, marching along the coast with all the speed they could, they directed their course towards Golpho Triste, the common refuge of the pirates. Being upon his journey, and all very hungry and thirsty, as is usual in desert places, they were pursued by a troop of an hundred Spaniards. Brasiliano, perceiving their imminent danger, encouraged his companions, telling them they were better soldiers, and ought rather to die under their arms fighting, as it became men of courage, than surrender to the Spaniards, who would take away their lives with the utmost torments. The pirates were but thirty; yet, seeing their brave commander oppose the enemy with such courage, resolved to do the like: hereupon they faced the troop of Spaniards, and discharged their muskets on them so dextrously, that they killed one horseman almost with every shot. The fight continued for an hour, till at last the Spaniards were put to flight. They stripped the dead, and took from them what was most for their use; such as were also not quite dead they dispatched with the ends of their muskets.

Having vanquished the enemy, they mounted on horses they found in the field, and continued their journey; Brasiliano having lost but two of his companions in this bloody fight, and had two wounded. Prosecuting their way, before they came to the port they spied a boat at anchor from Campechy, well manned, protecting a few canoes that were lading wood: hereupon they sent six of their men to watch them, who next morning, by a wile, possessed themselves of the canoes. Having given notice to their companions, they boarded them, and also took the little man-of-war, their convoy. Being thus masters of this fleet, they wanted only provisions, of which they found little aboard those vessels: but this defect was supplied by the horses, which they killed, and salted with salt, which by good fortune the wood-cutters had brought with them, with which they supported themselves till they could get better.

They took also another ship going from New Spain to Maracaibo, laden with divers sorts of merchandise and pieces of eight, designed to buy cocoa-nuts for their lading home: all these they carried to Jamaica, where they safely arrived, and, according to custom, wasted all in a few days in taverns, giving themselves to all manner of debauchery. Such of these pirates will spend two or three thousand pieces of eight in a night, not leaving themselves a good shirt to wear in the morning. My own master would buy sometimes a pipe of wine, and, placing it in the street, would force those that passed by to drink with him, threatening also to pistol them if they would not. He would do the like with barrels of beer or ale; and very often he would throw these liquors about the streets, and wet peoples' clothes without regarding whether he spoiled their apparel.

Among themselves these pirates are very liberal: if any one has lost all, which often happens in their manner of life, they freely give him of what they have. In taverns and alehouses they have great credit; but at Jamaica they ought not to run very deep in debt, seeing the inhabitants there easily sell one another for debt. This happened to my patron, to be sold for a debt of a tavern wherein he had spent the greatest part of his money. This man had, within three months before, three thousand pieces of eight in ready cash, all which he wasted in that little time, and became as poor as I have told you.

But to return Brasiliano, after having spent all, was forced to go to sea again to seek his fortune. He set forth towards the coast of Campechy, his common rendezvous: fifteen days after his arrival, he put himself into a canoe to espy the port of that city, and see if he could rob any Spanish vessel; but his fortune was so bad, that both he and all his men were taken and carried before the governor, who immediately cast them into a dungeon, intending to hang them every one; and doubtless he had done so, but for a stratagem of Brasiliano, which saved their lives. He wrote a letter to the governor, in the names of other pirates that were abroad at sea, telling them he should have a care how he used those persons he had in custody; for if he hurt them in the least, they swore they would never give quarter to any Spaniard that should fall into their hands.

These pirates having been often at Campechy, and other places of the West Indies in the Spanish dominions, the governor feared what mischief their companions abroad might do, if he should punish them. Hereupon he released them, exacting only an oath on them that they would leave their exercise of piracy for ever; and withal he sent them as common mariners, in the galleons, to Spain. They got in this voyage, all together, five hundred pieces of eight; so that they tarried not long there after their arrival. Providing themselves with necessaries, they returned to Jamaica, from whence they set forth again to sea, committing greater robberies and cruelties than before; but especially abusing the poor Spaniards, who fell into their hands, with all sorts of cruelty.

The Spaniards, finding they could gain nothing on these people, nor diminish their number, daily resolved to lessen the number of their trading ships. But neither was this of any service; for the pirates, finding few ships at sea, began to gather into companies, and to land on their dominions, ruining cities, towns, and villages; pillaging, burning, and carrying away as much as they could.

The first pirate who began these invasions by land was Lewis Scot, who sacked the city of Campechy, which he almost ruined, robbing and destroying all he could; and after he had put it to an excessive ransom, he left it. After Scot came another named Mansvelt, who invaded Granada, and penetrated even to the South Sea; till at last, for want of provision, he was forced to go back. He assaulted the isle of St. Catherine, which he took, with a few prisoners. These directed him to Carthagena, a principal city in Neuva Granada. But the bold attempts and actions of John Davis, born at Jamaica, ought not to be forgotten, being some of the most remarkable; especially his rare prudence and valour showed in the fore-mentioned kingdom of Granada. This pirate, having long cruised in the Gulf of Pocatauro, on the ships expected to Carthagena, bound for Nicaragua, and not meeting any of them, resolved at last to land in Nicaragua, leaving his ship hid on the coast.

This design he soon executed; for taking eighty men out of ninety, which he had in all—and the rest he left to keep the ship—he divided them equally into three canoes. His intent was to rob the churches, and rifle the houses of the chief citizens of Nicaragua. Thus in the dark night they entered the river leading to that city, rowing in their canoes; by day they hid themselves and boats under the branches of trees, on the banks, which grow very thick along the river-sides in those countries, and along the sea-coast. Being arrived at the city the third night, the sentinel, who kept the post of the river, thought them to be fishermen that had been fishing in the lake: and most of the pirates understanding Spanish, he doubted not, as soon as he heard them speak. They had in their company an Indian who had run away from his master, who would have enslaved him unjustly. He went first ashore, and instantly killed the sentinel: this done, they entered the city, and went directly to three or four houses of the chief citizens, where they knocked softly. These, believing them to be friends, opened the doors; and the pirates, suddenly possessing themselves of the houses, stole all the money and plate they could find. Nor did they spare the churches and most sacred things; all of which were pillaged and profaned, without any respect or veneration.

Meanwhile, great cries and lamentations were heard of some who had escaped them; so that the whole city was in an uproar, and all the citizens rallied in order, to a defence; which the pirates perceiving, they instantly fled, carrying away their booty, and some prisoners: these they led away, that if any of them should be taken by the Spaniards, they might use them for ransom. Thus they got to their ship, and with all speed put to sea, forcing the prisoners, before they let them go, to procure them as much flesh as was necessary for their voyage to Jamaica. But no sooner had they weighed anchor, when they saw a troop of about five hundred Spaniards, all well armed, at the sea-side: against these they let fly several guns, wherewith they forced them to quit the sands, and retire, with no small regret to see these pirates carry away so much plate of their churches and houses, though distant at least forty leagues from the sea.

These pirates got, on this occasion, above four thousand pieces of eight in money, besides much plate, and many jewels; in all, to the value of fifty thousand pieces of eight, or more: with all this they arrived at Jamaica soon after. But this sort of people being never long masters of their money, they were soon constrained to seek more by the same means; and Captain John Davis, presently after his return, was chosen admiral of seven or eight vessels, he being now esteemed an able conductor for such enterprises. He began his new command by directing his fleet to the north of Cuba, there to wait for the fleet from New Spain; but missing his design, they determined for Florida. Being arrived there, they landed their men, and sacked a small city named St. Augustine of Florida. The castle had a garrison of two hundred men, but could not prevent the pillage of the city, they effecting it without the least damage from the soldiers or townsmen.

Chapter VI

Of the origin of Francis Lolonois, and the beginning of his robberies.

FRANCIS LOLONOIS was a native of that territory in France which is called Les Sables d'Olone, or The Sands of Olone. In his youth he was transported to the Caribbee islands, in quality of servant, or slave, according to custom; of which we have already spoken. Being out of his time, he came to Hispaniola; here he joined for some time with the hunters, before he began his robberies upon the Spaniards, which I shall now relate, till his unfortunate death.

At first he made two or three voyages as a common mariner, wherein he behaved himself so courageously as to gain the favour of the governor of Tortuga, Monsieur de la Place; insomuch that he gave him a ship, in which he might seek his fortune, which was very favourable to him at first; for in a short time he got great riches. But his cruelties against the Spaniards were such, that the fame of them made him so well known through the Indies, that the Spaniards, in his time, would choose rather to die, or sink fighting, than surrender, knowing they should have no mercy at his hands. But Fortune, being seldom constant, after some time turned her back; for in a huge storm he lost his ship on the coast of Campechy. The men were all saved, but coming upon dry land, the Spaniards pursued them, and killed the greatest part, wounding also Lolonois. Not knowing how to escape, he saved his life by a stratagem; mingling sand with the blood of his wounds, with which besmearing his face, and other parts of his body, and hiding himself dextrously among the dead, he continued there till the Spaniards quitted the field.

They being gone, he retired to the woods, and bound up his wounds as well as he could. These being pretty well healed, he took his way to Campechy, having disguised himself in a Spanish habit; here he enticed certain slaves, to whom he promised liberty if they would obey him and trust to his conduct. They accepted his promises, and stealing a canoe, they went to sea with him. Now the Spaniards, having made several of his companions prisoners, kept them close in a dungeon, while Lolonois went about the town and saw what passed. These were often asked, "What is become of your captain?" To whom they constantly answered, "He is dead:" which rejoiced the Spaniards, who made bonfires, and, knowing nothing to the contrary, gave thanks to God for their deliverance from such a cruel pirate. Lolonois, having seen these rejoicings for his death, made haste to escape, with the slaves above-mentioned, and came safe to Tortuga, the common refuge of all sorts of wickedness, and the seminary, as it were, of pirates and thieves. Though now his fortune was low, yet he got another ship with craft and subtlety, and in it twenty-one men. Being well provided with arms and necessaries, he set forth for Cuba, on the south whereof is a small village, called De los Cayos. The inhabitants drive a great trade in tobacco, sugar, and hides, and all in boats, not being able to use ships, by reason of the little depth of that sea.

Lolonois was persuaded he should get here some considerable prey; but by the good fortune of some fishermen who saw him, and the mercy of God, they escaped him: for the inhabitants of the town dispatched immediately a vessel overland to the Havannah, complaining that Lolonois was come to destroy them with two canoes. The governor could very hardly believe this, having received letters from Campechy that he was dead: but, at their importunity, he sent a ship to their relief, with ten guns, and ninety men, well armed; giving them this express command, "that they should not return into his presence without having totally destroyed those pirates." To this effect he gave them a negro to serve for a hangman, and orders, "that they should immediately hang every one of the pirates, excepting Lolonois, their captain, whom they should bring alive to the Havannah." This ship arrived at Cayos, of whose coming the pirates were advertised beforehand, and instead of flying, went to seek it in the river Estera, where she rode at anchor. The pirates seized some fishermen, and forced them by night to show them the entry of the port, hoping soon to obtain a greater vessel than their two canoes, and thereby to mend their fortune. They arrived, after two in the morning, very nigh the ship; and the watch on board the ship asking them, whence they came, and if they had seen any pirates abroad? They caused one of the prisoners to answer, they had seen no pirates, nor anything else. Which answer made them believe that they were fled upon hearing of their coming.

But they soon found the contrary, for about break of day the pirates assaulted the vessel on both sides, with their two canoes, with such vigour, that though the Spaniards behaved themselves as they ought, and made as good defence as they could, making some use of their great guns, yet they were forced to surrender, being beaten by the pirates, with sword in hand, down under the hatches. From hence Lolonois commanded them to be brought up, one by one, and in this order caused their heads to be struck off: among the rest came up the negro, designed to be the pirates' executioner; this fellow implored mercy at his hands very dolefully, telling Lolonois he was constituted hangman of that ship, and if he would spare him, he would tell him faithfully all that he should desire. Lolonois, making him confess what he thought fit, commanded him to be murdered with the rest. Thus he cruelly and barbarously put them all to death, reserving only one alive, whom he sent back to the governor of the Havannah, with this message in writing: "I shall never henceforward give quarter to any Spaniard whatsoever; and I have great hopes I shall execute on your own person the very same punishment I have done upon them you sent against me. Thus I have retaliated the kindness you designed to me and my companions." The governor, much troubled at this sad news, swore, in the presence of many, that he would never grant quarter to any pirate that should fall into his hands. But the citizens of the Havannah desired him not to persist in the execution of that rash and rigorous oath, seeing the pirates would certainly take occasion from thence to do the same, and they had an hundred times more opportunity of revenge than he; that being necessitated to get their livelihood by fishery, they should hereafter always be in danger of their lives. By these reasons he was persuaded to bridle his anger, and remit the severity of his oath.

Now Lolonois had got a good ship, but very few provisions and people in it; to purchase both which, he resolved to cruise from one port to another. Doing thus, for some time, without success, he determined to go to the port of Maracaibo. Here he surprised a ship laden with plate, and other merchandises, outward bound, to buy cocoa-nuts. With this prize he returned to Tortuga, where he was received with joy by the inhabitants; they congratulating his happy success, and their own private interest. He stayed not long there, but designed to equip a fleet sufficient to transport five hundred men, and necessaries. Thus provided, he resolved to pillage both cities, towns, and villages, and finally, to take Maracaibo itself. For this purpose he knew the island of Tortuga would afford him many resolute and courageous men, fit for such enterprises: besides, he had in his service several prisoners well acquainted with the ways and places designed upon.

Chapter VII

Lolonois equips a fleet to land upon the Spanish islands of America, with intent to rob, sack and burn whatsoever he met with.

OF this design Lolonois giving notice to all the pirates, whether at home or abroad, he got together, in a little while, above four hundred men; beside which, there was then in Tortuga another pirate, named Michael de Basco, who, by his piracy, had got riches sufficient to live at ease, and go no more abroad; having, withal, the office of major of the island. But seeing the great preparations that Lolonois made for this expedition, he joined him, and offered him, that if he would make him his chief captain by land (seeing he knew the country very well, and all its avenues) he would share in his fortunes, and go with him. They agreed upon articles to the great joy of Lolonois, knowing that Basco had done great actions in Europe, and had the repute of a good soldier. Thus they all embarked in eight vessels, that of Lolonois being the greatest, having ten guns of indifferent carriage.

All things being ready, and the whole company on board, they set sail together about the end of April, being, in all, six hundred and sixty persons. They steered for that part called Bayala, north of Hispaniola: here they took into their company some French hunters, who voluntarily offered themselves, and here they provided themselves with victuals and necessaries for their voyage.

From hence they sailed again the last of July, and steered directly to the eastern cape of the isle called Punta d'Espada. Hereabouts espying a ship from Puerto Rico, bound for New Spain, laden with cocoa-nuts, Lolonois commanded the rest of the fleet to wait for him near Savona, on the east of

Cape Punta d'Espada, he alone intending to take the said vessel. The Spaniards, though they had been in sight full two hours, and knew them to be pirates, yet would not flee, but prepared to fight, being well armed, and provided. The combat lasted three hours, and then they surrendered. This ship had sixteen guns, and fifty fighting men aboard: they found in her 120,000 weight of cocoa, 40,000 pieces of eight, and the value of 10,000 more in jewels. Lolonois sent the vessel presently to Tortuga to be unladed, with orders to return as soon as possible to Savona, where he would wait for them: meanwhile, the rest of the fleet being arrived at Savona, met another Spanish vessel coming from Coman, with military provisions to Hispaniola, and money to pay the garrisons there. This vessel they also took, without any resistance, though mounted with eight guns. In it were 7,000 weight of powder, a great number of muskets, and like things, with 12,000 pieces of eight.

These successes encouraged the pirates, they seeming very lucky beginnings, especially finding their fleet pretty well recruited in a little time: for the first ship arriving at Tortuga, the governor ordered it to be instantly unladen, and soon after sent back, with fresh provisions, and other necessaries, to Lolonois. This ship he chose for himself, and gave that which he commanded to his comrade, Anthony du Puis. Being thus recruited with men in lieu of them he had lost in taking the prizes, and by sickness, he found himself in a good condition to set sail for Maracaibo, in the province of Neuva Venezuela, in the latitude of 12 deg. 10 min. north. This island is twenty leagues long, and twelve broad. To this port also belong the islands of Onega and Monges. The east side thereof is called Cape St. Roman, and the western side Cape of Caquibacoa: the gulf is called, by some, the Gulf of Venezuela, but the pirates usually call it the Bay of Maracaibo.

At the entrance of this gulf are two islands extending from east to west; that towards the east is called Isla de las Vigilias, or the Watch Isle; because in the middle is a high hill, on which stands a watch-house. The other is called Isla de la Palomas, or the Isle of Pigeons. Between these two islands runs a little sea, or rather lake of fresh water, sixty leagues long, and thirty broad; which disgorging itself into the ocean, dilates itself about the said two islands. Between them is the best passage for ships, the channel being no broader than the flight of a great gun, of about eight pounds. On the Isle of Pigeons standeth a castle, to impede the entry of vessels, all being necessitated to come very nigh the castle, by reason of two banks of sand on the other side, with only fourteen feet water. Many other banks of sand there are in this lake; as that called El Tablazo, or the Great Table, no deeper than ten feet, forty leagues within the lake; others there are, that have no more than six, seven, or eight feet in depth: all are very dangerous, especially to mariners unacquainted with them. West hereof is the city of Maracaibo, very pleasant to the view, its houses being built along the shore, having delightful prospects all round: the city may contain three or four thousand persons, slaves included, all which make a town of reasonable bigness. There are judged to be about eight hundred persons able to bear arms, all Spaniards. Here are one parish church, well built and adorned, four monasteries, and one hospital. The city is governed by a deputy governor, substituted by the governor of the Caraccas. The trade here exercised is mostly in hides and tobacco. The inhabitants possess great numbers of cattle, and many plantations, which extend thirty leagues in the country, especially towards the great town of Gibraltar, where are gathered great quantities of cocoa-nuts, and all other garden fruits, which serve for the regale and sustenance of the inhabitants of Maracaibo, whose territories are much drier than those of Gibraltar. Hither those of Maracaibo send great quantities of flesh, they making returns in oranges, lemons, and other fruits; for the inhabitants of Gibraltar want flesh, their fields not being capable of feeding cows or sheep.

Before Maracaibo is a very spacious and secure port, wherein may be built all sorts of vessels, having great convenience of timber, which may be transported thither at little charge. Nigh the town lies also a small island called Borrica, where they feed great numbers of goats, which cattle the inhabitants use more for their skins than their flesh or milk; they slighting these two, unless while they are tender and young kids. In the fields are fed some sheep, but of a very small size. In some islands of the lake, and in other places hereabouts, are many savage Indians, called by the Spaniards bravoes, or wild: these could never be reduced by the Spaniards, being brutish, and untameable. They dwell mostly towards the west side of the lake, in little huts built on trees growing in the water; so to keep themselves from innumerable mosquitoes, or gnats, which infest and torment them night and day. To the east of the said lake are whole towns of fishermen, who likewise live in huts built on trees, as the former. Another reason of this dwelling, is the frequent inundations; for after great rains, the land is often overflown for two or three leagues, there being no less than twenty-five great rivers that feed this lake. The town of Gibraltar is also frequently drowned by these, so that the inhabitants are constrained to retire to their plantations.

Gibraltar, situate at the side of the lake about forty leagues within it, receives its provisions of flesh, as has been said, from Maracaibo. The town is inhabited by about 1,500 persons, whereof four hundred may bear arms; the greatest part of them keep shops, wherein they exercise one trade or another. In the adjacent fields are numerous plantations of sugar and cocoa, in which are many tall and beautiful trees, of whose timber houses may be built, and ships. Among these are many handsome and proportionable cedars, seven or eight feet about, of which they can build boats and ships, so

44

as to bear only one great sail; such vessels being called piraguas. The whole country is well furnished with rivers and brooks, very useful in droughts, being then cut into many little channels to water their fields and plantations. They plant also much tobacco, well esteemed in Europe, and for its goodness is called there tobacco de sacerdotes, or priest's tobacco. They enjoy nigh twenty leagues of jurisdiction, which is bounded by very high mountains perpetually covered with snow. On the other side of these mountains is situate a great city called Merida, to which the town of Gibraltar is subject. All merchandise is carried hence to the aforesaid city on mules, and that but at one season of the year, by reason of the excessive cold in those high mountains. On the said mules returns are made in flour of meal, which comes from towards Peru, by the way of Estaffe.

Thus far I thought good to make a short description of the lake of Maracaibo, that my reader might the better comprehend what I shall say concerning the actions of pirates in this place, as follows.

Lolonois arriving at the gulf of Venezuela, cast anchor with his whole fleet out of sight of the Vigilia or Watch Isle; next day very early he set sail thence with all his ships for the lake of Maracaibo, where they cast anchor again; then they landed their men, with design to attack first the fortress that commanded the bar, therefore called de la barra. This fort consists only of several great baskets of earth placed on a rising ground, planted with sixteen great guns, with several other heaps of earth round about for covering their men: the pirates having landed a league off this fort, advanced by degrees towards it; but the governor having espied their landing, had placed an ambuscade to cut them off behind, while he should attack them in front. This the pirates discovered, and getting before, they defeated it so entirely, that not a man could retreat to the castle: this done, Lolonois, with his companions, advanced immediately to the fort, and after a fight of almost three hours, with the usual desperation of this sort of people, they became masters thereof, without any other arms than swords and pistols: while they were fighting, those who were the routed ambuscade, not being able to get into the castle, retired into Maracaibo in great confusion and disorder, crying "The pirates will presently be here with two thousand men and more." The city having formerly been taken by this kind of people, and sacked to the uttermost, had still an idea of that misery; so that upon these dismal news they endeavoured to escape towards Gibraltar in their boats and canoes, carrying with them all the goods and money they could. Being come to Gibraltar, they told how the fortress was taken, and nothing had been saved, nor any persons escaped.

The castle thus taken by the pirates, they presently signified to the ships their victory, that they should come farther in without fear of danger: the rest of that day was spent in ruining and demolishing the said castle. They nailed the guns, and burnt as much as they could not carry away, burying the dead, and sending on board the fleet the wounded. Next day, very early, they weighed anchor, and steered altogether towards Maracaibo, about six leagues distant from the fort; but the wind failing that day, they could advance little, being forced to expect the tide. Next morning they came in sight of the town, and prepared for landing under the protection of their own guns, fearing the Spaniards might have laid an ambuscade in the woods: they put their men into canoes, brought for that purpose, and landed where they thought most convenient, shooting still furiously with their great guns: of those in the canoes, half only went ashore, the other half remained aboard; they fired from the ships as fast as possible, towards the woody part of the shore, but could discover nobody; then they entered the town, whose inhabitants, as I told you, were retired to the woods, and Gibraltar, with their wives, children, and families. Their houses they left well provided with victuals, as flour, bread, pork, brandy, wines, and poultry, with these the pirates fell to making good cheer, for in four weeks before they had no opportunity of filling their stomachs with such plenty.

They instantly possessed themselves of the best houses in the town, and placed sentinels wherever they thought convenient; the great church served them for their main guard. Next day they sent out an hundred and sixty men to find out some of the inhabitants in the woods thereabouts; these returned the same night, bringing with them 20,000 pieces of eight, several mules laden with household goods and merchandise, and twenty prisoners, men, women, and children. Some of these were put to the rack, to make them confess where they had hid the rest of the goods; but they could extort very little from them. Lolonois, who valued not murdering, though in cold blood, ten or twelve Spaniards, drew his cutlass, and hacked one to pieces before the rest, saying, "If you do not confess and declare where you have hid the rest of your goods, I will do the like to all your companions." At last, amongst these horrible cruelties and inhuman threats, one promised to show the place where the rest of the Spaniards were hid; but those that were fled, having intelligence of it, changed place, and buried the remnant of their riches underground, so that the pirates could not find them out, unless some of their own party should reveal them; besides, the Spaniards flying from one place to another every day, and often changing woods, were jealous even of each other, so as the father durst scarce trust his own son.

After the pirates had been fifteen days in Maracaibo, they resolved for Gibraltar; but the inhabitants having received intelligence thereof, and that they intended afterwards to go to Merida, gave notice of it to the governor there, who was a valiant soldier, and had been an officer in Flanders. His answer was, "he would have them take no care, for he hoped in a little while to exterminate the said pirates." Whereupon he came to Gibraltar with four hundred men well armed, ordering at the same time the inhabitants to put themselves in arms, so that in all he made eight hundred fighting men. With the same speed he raised a battery toward the sea, mounted with twenty guns, covered with great baskets of earth: another battery he placed in another place, mounted with eight guns. This done, he barricaded a narrow passage to the town through which the pirates must pass, opening at the same time another through much dirt and mud into the wood totally unknown to the pirates.

The pirates, ignorant of these preparations, having embarked all their prisoners and booty, took their way towards Gibraltar. Being come in sight of the place, they saw the royal standard hanging forth, and that those of the town designed to defend their houses. Lolonois seeing this, called a council of war what they ought to do, telling his officers and mariners, "That the difficulty of the enterprise was very great, seeing the Spaniards had had so much time to put themselves in a posture of defence, and had got a good body of men together, with much ammunition; but notwithstanding," said he, "have a good courage; we must either defend ourselves like good soldiers, or lose our lives with all the riches we have got. Do as I shall do who am your captain: at other times we have fought with fewer men than we have in our company at present, and yet we have overcome greater numbers than there possibly can be in this town: the more they are, the more glory and the greater riches we shall gain." The pirates supposed that all the riches of the inhabitants of Maracaibo were transported to Gibraltar, or at least the greatest part. After this speech, they all promised to follow, and obey him. Lolonois made answer, "'Tis well; but know ye, withal, that the first man who shall show any fear, or the least apprehension thereof, I will pistol him with my own hands."

With this resolution they cast anchor nigh the shore, near three-quarters of a league from the town: next day before sun-rising, they landed three hundred and eighty men well provided, and armed every one with a cutlass, and one or two pistols, and sufficient powder and bullet for thirty charges. Here they all shook hands in testimony of good courage, and began their march, Lolonois speaking thus, "Come, my brethren, follow me, and have good courage." They followed their guide, who, believing he led them well, brought them to the way which the governor had barricaded. Not being able to pass that way, they went to the other newly made in the wood among the mire, which the Spaniards could shoot into at pleasure; but the pirates, full of courage, cut down the branches of trees and threw them on the way, that they might not stick in the dirt. Meanwhile, those of Gibraltar fired with their great guns so furiously, they could scarce hear nor see for the noise and smoke. Being passed the wood, they came on firm ground, where they met with a battery of six guns, which immediately the Spaniards discharged upon them, all loaded with small bullets and pieces of iron; and the Spaniards sallying forth, set upon them with such fury, as caused the pirates to give way, few of them caring to advance towards the fort, many of them being already killed and wounded. This made them go back to seek another way; but the Spaniards having cut down many trees to hinder the passage, they could find none, but were forced to return to that they had left. Here the Spaniards continued to fire as before, nor would they sally out of their batteries to attack them any more. Lolonois and his companions not being able to grimp up the baskets of earth, were compelled to use an old stratagem, wherewith at last they deceived and overcame the Spaniards.

Lolonois retired suddenly with all his men, making show as if he fled; hereupon the Spaniards crying out "They flee, they flee, let us follow them," sallied forth with great disorder to the pursuit. Being drawn to some distance from the batteries, which was the pirates only design, they turned upon them unexpectedly with sword in hand, and killed above two hundred men; and thus fighting their way through those who remained, they possessed themselves of the batteries. The Spaniards that remained abroad, giving themselves over for lost, fled to the woods: those in the battery of eight guns surrendered themselves, obtaining quarter for their lives. The pirates being now become masters of the town, pulled down the Spanish colours and set up their own, taking prisoners as many as they could find. These they carried to the great church, where they raised a battery of several great guns, fearing lest the Spaniards that were fled should rally, and come upon them again; but next day, being all fortified, their fears were over. They gathered the dead to bury them, being above five hundred Spaniards, besides the wounded in the town, and those that died of their wounds in the woods. The pirates had also above one hundred and fifty prisoners, and nigh five hundred slaves, many women and children.

Of their own companions only forty were killed, and almost eighty wounded, whereof the greatest part died through the bad air, which brought fevers and other illness. They put the slain Spaniards into two great boats, and carrying them a quarter of a league to sea, they sunk the boats; this done, they gathered all the plate, household stuff, and merchandise they could, or thought convenient to carry away. The Spaniards who had anything left had hid it carefully: but the unsatisfied pirates, not contented with the riches they had got, sought for more goods and merchandise, not sparing those who lived in the fields, such as hunters and planters. They had scarce been eighteen days on the place, when the greatest part of the prisoners died for hunger. For in the town were few provisions, especially of flesh, though they had some, but no sufficient quantity of flour of meal, and this the pirates had taken for themselves, as they also took the swine, cows, sheep, and poultry, without allowing any share to the poor prisoners; for these they only provided some small quantity of mules' and asses' flesh; and many who could not eat of that loathsome provision died for hunger, their stomachs not being accustomed to such sustenance. Of the prisoners many also died under the torment they sustained to make them discover their money or jewels; and of these, some had none, nor knew of none, and others denying what they knew, endured such horrible deaths.

Finally, after having been in possession of the town four entire weeks, they sent four of the prisoners to the Spaniards that were fled to the woods, demanding of them a ransom for not burning the town. The sum demanded was 10,000 pieces of eight, which if not sent, they threatened to reduce it to ashes. For bringing in this money, they allowed them only two days; but the Spaniards not having been able to gather so punctually such a sum, the pirates fired many parts of the town; whereupon the inhabitants begged them to help quench the fire, and the ransom should be readily paid. The pirates condescended, helping as much as they could to stop the fire; but, notwithstanding all their best endeavours, one part of the town was ruined, especially the church belonging to the monastery was burnt down. After they had received the said sum, they carried aboard all the riches they had got, with a great number of slaves which had not paid the ransom; for all the prisoners had sums of money set upon them, and the slaves were also commanded to be redeemed. Hence they returned to Maracaibo, where being arrived, they found a general consternation in the whole city, to which they sent three or four prisoners to tell the governor and inhabitants, "they should bring them 30,000 pieces of eight aboard their ships, for a ransom of their houses, otherwise they should be sacked anew and burnt."

Among these debates a party of pirates came on shore, and carried away the images, pictures, and bells of the great church, aboard the fleet. The Spaniards who were sent to demand the sum aforesaid returned, with orders to make some agreement; who concluded with the pirates to give for their ransom and liberty 20,000 pieces of eight, and five hundred cows, provided that they should commit no farther hostilities, but depart thence presently after payment of money and cattle. The one and the other being delivered, the whole fleet set sail, causing great joy to the inhabitants of Maracaibo, to see themselves quit of them: but three days after they renewed their fears with admiration, seeing the pirates appear again, and re-enter the port with all their ships: but these apprehensions vanished, upon hearing one of the pirate's errand, who came ashore from Lolonois, "to demand a skilful pilot to conduct one of the greatest ships over the dangerous bank that lieth at the very entry of the lake." Which petition, or rather command, was instantly granted.

They had now been full two months in those towns, wherein they committed those cruel and insolent actions we have related. Departing thence, they took their course to Hispaniola, and arrived there in eight days, casting anchor in a port called Isla de la Vacca, or Cow Island. This island is inhabited by French bucaniers, who mostly sell the flesh they hunt to pirates and others, who now and then put in there to victual, or trade. Here they unladed their whole cargazon of riches, the usual storehouse of the pirates being commonly under the shelter of the bucaniers. Here they made a dividend of all their prizes and gains, according to the order and degree of every one, as has been mentioned before. Having made an exact calculation of all their plunder, they found in ready money 260,000 pieces of eight: this being divided, every one received for his share in money, as also in silk, linen, and other commodities, to the value of above 100 pieces of eight. Those who had been wounded received their first part, after the rate mentioned before, for the loss of their limbs: then they weighed all the plate uncoined, reckoning ten pieces of eight to a pound; the jewels were prized indifferently, either too high or too low, by reason of their ignorance: this done, every one was put to his oath again, that he had not smuggled anything from the common stock. Hence they proceeded to the dividend of the shares of such as were dead in battle, or otherwise: these shares were given to their friends, to be kept entire for them, and to be delivered in due time to their nearest relations, or their apparent lawful heirs.

The whole dividend being finished, they set sail for Tortuga: here they arrived a month after, to the great joy of most of the island; for as to the common pirates, in three weeks they had scarce any money left, having spent it all in things of little value, or lost it at play. Here had arrived, not long before them, two French ships, with wine and brandy, and suchlike commodities; whereby these liquors, at the arrival of the pirates, were indifferent cheap. But this lasted not long, for soon after they were enhanced extremely, a gallon of brandy being sold for four pieces of eight. The governor of the island bought of the pirates the whole cargo of the ship laden with cocoa, giving for that rich commodity scarce the twentieth part of its worth. Thus they made shift to lose and spend the riches they had got, in much less time than they were purchased: the taverns and stews, according to the custom of pirates, got the greatest part; so that, soon after, they were forced to seek more by the same unlawful means they had got the former.

Chapter VIII

Lolonois makes new preparations to make the city of St. James de Leon; as also that of Nicaragua; where he miserably perishes.

LOLONOIS had got great repute at Tortuga by this last voyage, because he brought home such considerable profit; and now he need take no great care to gather men to serve under him, more coming in voluntarily than he could employ; every one reposing such confidence in his conduct that they judged it very safe to expose themselves, in his company, to the greatest dangers. He resolved therefore a second voyage to the parts of Nicaragua, to pillage there as many towns as he could.

Having published his new preparations, he had all his men together at the time, being about seven hundred. Of these he put three hundred aboard the ship he took at Maracaibo, and the rest in five other vessels of lesser burthen; so that they were in all six ships. The first port they went to was Bayaha in Hispaniola, to victual the fleet, and take in provisions; which done, they steered their course to a port called Matamana, on the south side of Cuba, intending to take here all the canoes they could; these coasts being frequented by the fishers of tortoises, who carry them hence to the Havannah. They took as many of them, to the great grief of those miserable people, as they thought necessary; for they had great use for these small bottoms, by reason the port they designed for had not depth enough for ships of any burthen. Hence they took their course towards the cape Gracias à Dios on the continent, in latitude 15 deg. north, one hundred leagues from the Island de los Pinos. Being at sea, they were taken with a sad and tedious calm, and, by the agitation of the waves alone, were thrown into the gulf of Honduras: here they laboured hard in vain to regain what they had lost, both the waters and the winds being contrary; besides, the ship wherein Lolonois was embarked could not follow the rest; and what was worse, they wanted provisions. Hereupon, they were forced to put into the first port they could reach, to revictual: so they entered with their canoes into the river Xagua, inhabited by Indians, whom they totally destroyed, finding great quantities of millet, and many hogs and hens: not contented with which, they determined to remain there till the bad weather was over, and to pillage all the towns and villages along the coast of the gulf. Thus they passed from one place to another, seeking still more provisions, with which they were not sufficiently supplied. Having searched and rifled many villages, where they found no great matter, they came at last to Puerto Cavallo: here the Spaniards have two storehouses to keep the merchandises that are brought from the inner parts of the country, till the arrival of the ships. There was then in the port a Spanish ship of twenty-four guns, and sixteen pedreros or mortar-pieces: this ship was immediately seized by the pirates, and then drawing nigh the shore, they landed, and burnt the two storehouses, with all the rest of the houses there. Many inhabitants likewise they took prisoners, and committed upon them the most inhuman cruelties that ever heathens invented; putting them to the cruellest tortures they could devise. It was the custom of Lolonois, that having tormented persons not confessing, he would instantly cut them in pieces with his hanger, and pull out their tongues, desiring to do so, if possible, to every Spaniard in the world. It often happened that some of these miserable prisoners, being forced by the rack, would promise to discover the places where the fugitive Spaniards lay hid, which not being able afterwards to perform, they were put to more cruel deaths than they who were dead before.

The prisoners being all dead but two (whom they reserved to show them what they desired), they marched hence to the town of San Pedro, or St. Peter, ten or twelve leagues from Puerto Cavallo, being three hundred men, whom Lolonois led, leaving behind him Moses van Vin his lieutenant, to govern the rest in his absence. Being come three leagues on their way, they met with a troop of Spaniards, who lay in ambuscade for their coming: these they set upon, with all the courage imaginable, and at last totally defeated. Howbeit, they behaved themselves very manfully at first; but not being able to resist the fury of the pirates, they were forced to give way, and save themselves by flight, leaving many pirates dead in the place, some wounded, and some of their own party maimed, by the way. These Lolonois put to death without mercy, having asked them what questions he thought fit for his purpose.

There were still remaining some few prisoners not wounded; these were asked by Lolonois, if any more Spaniards did lie farther on in ambuscade? They answered, there were. Then being brought before him, one by one, he asked if there was no other way to town but that. This he did to avoid if possible those ambuscades. But they all constantly answered him they knew none. Having asked them all, and finding they could show him no other way, Lolonois grew outrageously passionate; so that he drew his cutlass, and with it cut open the breast of one of those poor Spaniards, and pulling out his heart began to bite and gnaw it with his teeth, like a ravenous wolf, saying to the rest, "I will serve you all alike, if you show me not another way."

Hereupon, those miserable wretches promised to show him another way, but withal, they told him, it was extremely difficult, and laborious. Thus to satisfy that cruel tyrant, they began to lead him and his army; but finding it not for his purpose as they had told him, he was forced to return to the former way, swearing with great choler and indignation, "Mort Dieu, les

Espagnols me le payeront. By God's death, the Spaniards shall pay me for this."

Next day he fell into another ambuscade, which he assaulted with such horrible fury, that in less than an hour's time he routed the Spaniards, and killed the greatest part of them. The Spaniards thought by these ambuscades better to destroy the pirates, assaulting them by degrees, and for this reason had posted themselves in several places. At last he met with a third ambuscade, where was placed a party stronger, and more advantageously, than the former: yet notwithstanding, the pirates, by continually throwing little fire-balls in great numbers, for some time, forced this party, as well as the former, to flee, and this with so great loss of men, that before they could reach the town, the greatest part of the Spaniards were either killed or wounded. There was but one path which led to the town, very well barricaded with good defences; and the rest of the town round was planted with shrubs called raqueltes, full of thorns very sharp pointed. This sort of fortification seemed stronger than the triangles used in Europe, when an army is of necessity to pass by the place of an enemy; it being almost impossible for the pirates to traverse those shrubs. The Spaniards posted behind the said defences, seeing the pirates come, began to ply them with their great guns; but these perceiving them ready to fire, used to stoop down, and when the shot was made, to fall upon the defendants with fire-balls and naked swords, killing many of the town: yet notwithstanding, not being able to advance any farther, they retired, for the present: then they renewed the attack with fewer men than before, and observing not to shoot till they were very nigh, they gave the Spaniards a charge so dextrously, that with every shot they killed an enemy.

The attack continuing thus eager on both sides till night, the Spaniards were compelled to hang forth a white flag, and desired to come to a parley: the only conditions they required were, "that the pirates should give the inhabitants quarter for two hours." This little time they demanded with intent to carry away and hide as much of their goods and riches as they could, and to fly to some other neighbouring town. Granting this article, they entered the town, and continued there the two hours, without committing the least hostility on the inhabitants; but no sooner was that time past, than Lolonois ordered that the inhabitants should be followed, and robbed of all they had carried away; and not only their goods, but their persons likewise to be made prisoners; though the greatest part of their merchandise and goods were so hid, as the pirates could not find them, except a few leathern sacks, filled with anil, or indigo.

Having stayed here a few days, and, according to their custom, committed most horrid insolences, they at last quitted the place, carrying away all they

53

possibly could, and reducing the town to ashes. Being come to the seaside, where they left a party of their own, they found these had been cruising upon the fishermen thereabouts, or who came that way from the river of Guatemala: in this river was also expected a ship from Spain. Finally, they resolved to go toward the islands on the other side of the gulf, there to cleanse and careen their vessels; but they left two canoes before the coast, or rather the mouth of the river of Guatemala, in order to take the ship, which, as I said, was expected from Spain.

But their chief intent in going hither was to seek provisions, knowing the tortoises of those places are excellent food. Being arrived, they divided themselves, each party choosing a fit post for that fishery. They undertook to knit nets with the rinds of certain trees called macoa, whereof they make also ropes and cables; so that no vessel can be in need of such things, if they can but find the said trees. There are also many places where they find pitch in so great abundance, that running down the sea-coasts, being melted by the sun, it congeals in the water in great heaps, like small islands. This pitch is not like that of Europe, but resembles, both in colour and shape, that froth of the sea called bitumen; but, in my judgment, this matter is nothing but wax mixed with sand, which stormy weather, and the rolling waves of great rivers hath cast into the sea; for in those parts are great quantities of bees who make their honey in trees, to the bodies of which the honeycomb being fixed, when tempests arise, they are torn away, and by the fury of the winds carried into the sea, as is said. Some naturalists say, that the honey and the wax are separated by the salt water; whence proceeds the good amber. This opinion seems the more probable, because the said amber tastes as wax doth.

But to return to my discourse. The pirates made in those islands all the haste they possibly could to equip their vessels, hearing that the Spanish ship was come which they expected. They spent some time cruising on the coasts of Jucatan, where inhabit many Indians, who seek for the said amber in those seas. And I shall here, by the by, make some short remarks on the manner of living of the Indians, and their religion.

They have now been above a hundred years under the Spaniards, to whom they performed all manner of services; for whensoever any of them needed a slave or servant, they sent for these to serve them as long as they pleased. By the Spaniards they were initiated in the principles of the Christian faith and religion, and they sent them every Sunday and holiday a priest to perform divine service among them; afterwards, for reasons not known, but certainly through temptations of the father of idolatry, the devil, they suddenly cast off the Christian religion, abusing the priest that was sent them: this provoked the Spaniards to punish them, by casting many of the chiefs into prison. Every one of those barbarians had, and hath still, a god to himself, whom he serves and worships. It is a matter of admiration, how they use a child newly born: as soon as it comes into the world, they carry it to the temple; here they make a hole, which they fill with ashes only, on which they place the child naked, leaving it there a whole night alone, not without great danger, nobody daring to come near it; meanwhile the temple is open on all sides, that all sorts of beasts may freely come in and out. Next day, the father, and relations of the infant, return to see if the track or step of any animal appears in the ashes: not finding any, they leave the child there till some beast has approached the infant, and left behind him the marks of his feet: to this animal, whatsoever it be, they consecrate the creature newly born, as to its god, which he is bound to worship all his life, esteeming the said beast his patron and protector. They offer to their gods sacrifices of fire, wherein they burn a certain gum called by them copal, whose smoke smells very deliciously. When the infant is grown up, the parents thereof tell him who he ought to worship, and serve, and honour as his own proper god. Then he goes to the temple, where he makes offerings to the said beast. Afterwards, if in the course of his life, any one injure him, or any evil happen to him, he complains to that beast, and sacrifices to it for revenge. Hence it often comes, that those who have done the injury of which he complains are bitten, killed, or otherwise hurt by such animals.

After this superstitious and idolatrous manner live those miserable and ignorant Indians that inhabit the islands of the gulf of Honduras; as also many of them on the continent of Jucatan, in the territories whereof are most excellent ports, where those Indians most commonly build their houses. These people are not very faithful to one another, and use strange ceremonies at their marriages. Whensoever any one pretends to marry a young damsel, he first applies himself to her father or nearest relation: he examines him nicely about the manner of cultivating their plantations, and other things at his pleasure. Having satisfied the questions of his father-in-law, he gives the young man a bow and arrow, with which he repairs to the young maid, and presents her with a garland of green leaves and sweet-smelling flowers; this she is obliged to put on her head, and lay aside that which she wore before, it being the custom for virgins to go perpetually crowned with flowers. This garland being received, and put on her head, every one of the relations and friends go to advise with others whether that marriage will be like to be happy or not; then they meet at the house of the damsel's father, where they drink of a liquor made of maize, or Indian wheat; and here, before the whole company, the father gives his daughter in marriage to the bridegroom. Next day the bride comes to her mother, and in her presence pulls off the garland, and tears it in pieces, with great cries and lamentations. Many other things I could relate of the manner of living and customs of those Indians, but I shall follow my discourse.

Our pirates therefore had many canoes of the Indians in the isle of Sambale, five leagues from the coasts of Jucatan. Here is great quantity of amber, but especially when any storm arises from towards the east; whence the waves bring many things, and very different. Through this sea no vessels can pass, unless very small, it being too shallow. In the lands that are surrounded by this sea, is found much Campechy wood, and other things that serve for dyeing, much esteemed in Europe, and would be more, if we had the skill of the Indians, who make a dye or tincture that never fades.

The pirates having been in that gulf three months, and receiving advice that the Spanish ship was come, hastened to the port where the ship lay at anchor unlading her merchandise, with design to assault her as soon as possible; but first they thought convenient to send away some of their boats to seek for a small vessel also expected very richly laden with plate, indigo, and cochineal. Meanwhile, the ship's crew having notice that the pirates designed upon them, prepared all things for a good defence, being mounted with forty-two guns, well furnished with arms and other necessaries, and one hundred and thirty fighting men. To Lolonois all this seemed but little, for he assaulted her with great courage, his own ship carrying but twenty-two guns, and having no more than a small saety or fly-boat for help: but the Spaniards defended themselves so well, as they forced the pirates to retire; but the smoke of the powder continuing thick, as a dark fog or mist, with four canoes well manned, they boarded the ship with great agility, and forced the Spaniards to surrender.

The ship being taken, they found not in her what they thought, being already almost unladen. All they got was only fifty bars of iron, a small parcel of paper, some earthen jars of wine, and other things of small importance.

Then Lolonois called a council of war, and told them, he intended for Guatemala: hereupon they divided into several sentiments, some liking the proposal, and others disliking it, especially a party of them who were but raw in those exercises, and who imagined at their setting forth from Tortuga that pieces of eight were gathered as easy as pears from a tree; but finding most things contrary to their expectation, they quitted the fleet, and returned; others affirmed they had rather starve than return home without a great deal of money.

But the major part judging the propounded voyage little to their purpose, separated from Lolonois and the rest: of these one Moses Vanclein was ringleader, captain of the ship taken at Puerto Cavallo: this fellow steered for Tortuga, to cruise to and fro in these seas. With him joined another comrade of his, by name Pierre le Picard, who seeing the rest leave Lolonois, thought fit to do the same. These runaways having thus parted company, steered homewards, coasting along the continent till they came to Costa Rica; here they landed a strong party nigh the river Veraguas, and marched in good order to the town of the same name: this they took and totally pillaged, though the Spaniards made a strong resistance. They brought away some of the inhabitants as prisoners, with all they had, which was of no great importance, by reason of the poverty of the place, which exerciseth no other trade than working in the mines, where some of the inhabitants constantly attend, while none seek for gold, but only slaves. These they compel to dig and wash the earth in the neighbouring rivers, where often they find pieces of gold as big as peas. The pirates gaining in this adventure but seven or eight pounds weight of gold, they returned, giving over the design to go to the town of Nata, situate on the coasts of the South Sea, whose inhabitants are rich merchants, and their slaves work in the mines of Veraguas; being deterred by the multitudes of Spaniards gathered on all sides to fall upon them, whereof they had timely advice.

Lolonois, thus left by his companions, remained alone in the gulf of Honduras. His ship being too great to get out at the reflux of those seas, there he sustained great want of provisions, so as they were constrained to go ashore every day to seek sustenance, and not finding anything else, they were forced to kill and eat monkeys, and other animals, such as they could find.

At last in the altitude of the cape of Gracias a Dios, near a certain little island called De las Pertas, his ship struck on a bank of sand, where it stuck so fast, as no art could get her off again, though they unladed all the guns, iron, and other weighty things as much as they could. Hereupon they were forced to break the ship in pieces, and with planks and nails build themselves a boat to get away; and while they are busy about it, I shall describe the said isles and their inhabitants.

The islands De las Pertas are inhabited by savage Indians, not having known or conversed with civil people: they are tall and very nimble, running almost as fast as horses; at diving also they are very dextrous and hardy. From the bottom of the sea I saw them take up an anchor of six hundredweight, tying a cable to it with great dexterity, and pulling it from a rock. Their arms are made of wood, without any iron point; but some instead thereof use a crocodile's tooth. They have no bows nor arrows, as the other Indians have, but their common weapon is a sort of lance a fathom and a half long. Here are many plantations surrounded with woods, whence they gather abundance of fruits, as potatoes, bananas, racoven, ananas, and many others. They have no houses to dwell in, as at other places in the Indies. Some say they eat human flesh, which is confirmed by what happened when Lolonois was there. Two of his companions, one a Frenchman and the other a Spaniard, went into the woods, where having straggled awhile, a troop of Indians pursued them. They defended themselves as well as they could with their swords, but at last were forced to flee. The nimble Frenchman escaped; but the Spaniard being not so swift, was taken and heard of no more. Some days after, twelve pirates set forth well armed to seek their companion, among whom was the Frenchman, who conducted them, and showed them the place where he left him; here they found that the Indians had kindled a fire, and at a small distance they found a man's bones well roasted, with some pieces of flesh ill scraped off the bones, and one hand, which had only two fingers remaining, whence they concluded they had roasted the poor Spaniard.

They marched on, seeking for Indians, and found a great number together, who endeavoured to escape, but they overtook some of them, and brought aboard their ships five men and four women; with these they took much pains to make themselves be understood, and to gain their affections, giving them trifles, as knives, beads, and the like; they gave them also victuals and drink, but nothing would they taste. It was also observable, that while they were prisoners, they spoke not one word to each other; so that seeing these poor Indians were much afraid, they presented them again with some small things, and let them go. When they parted, they made signs they would come again, but they soon forgot their benefactors, and were never heard of more; neither could any notice afterwards be had of these Indians, nor any others in the whole island, which made the pirates suspect that both those that were taken, and all the rest of the islanders, swam away by night to some little neighbouring islands, especially considering they could never set eyes on any Indian more, nor any boat or other vessel. Meanwhile the pirates were very desirous to see their long-boat finished out of the timber that struck on the sands; yet considering their work would be long, they began to cultivate some pieces of ground; here they sowed French beans, which ripened in six weeks, and many other fruits. They had good provision of Spanish wheat, bananas, racoven, and other things; with the wheat they made bread, and baked it in portable ovens, brought with them. Thus they feared not hunger in those desert places, employing themselves thus for five or six months; which past, and the long-boat finished, they resolved for the river of Nicaragua, to see if they could take some canoes, and return to the said islands for their companions that remained behind, by reason the boat could not hold so many men together; hereupon, to avoid disputes, they cast lots, determining who should go or stay.

The lot fell on one half of the people of the lost vessel, who embarked in the long-boat, and on the skiff which they had before, the other half remaining ashore. Lolonois having set sail, arrived in a few days at the river of Nicaragua: here that ill-fortune assailed him which of long time had been reserved for him, as a punishment due to the multitude of horrible crimes committed in his licentious and wicked life. Here he met with both Spaniards and Indians, who jointly setting upon him and his companions, the greatest part of the pirates were killed on the place. Lolonois, with those that remained alive, had much ado to escape aboard their boats: yet notwithstanding this great loss, he resolved not to return to those he had left at the isle of Pertas, without taking some boats, such as he looked for. To this effect he determined to go on to the coasts of Carthagena; but God Almighty, the time of His Divine justice being now come, had appointed the Indians of Darien to be the instruments and executioners thereof. These Indians of Darien are esteemed as bravoes, or wild savage Indians, by the neighbouring Spaniards, who never could civilize them. Hither Lolonois came (brought by his evil conscience that cried for punishment), thinking to act his cruelties; but the Indians within a few days after his arrival took him prisoner, and tore him in pieces alive, throwing his body limb by limb into the fire, and his ashes into the air, that no trace or memory might remain of such an infamous, inhuman creature. One of his companions gave me an exact account of this tragedy, affirming that himself had escaped the same punishment with the greatest difficulty; he believed also that many of his comrades, who were taken in that encounter by those Indians, were, as their cruel captain, torn in pieces and burnt alive. Thus ends the history, the life, and miserable death of that infernal wretch Lolonois, who full of horrid, execrable, and enormous deeds, and debtor to so much innocent blood, died by cruel and butcherly hands, such as his own were in the course of his life.

Those that remained in the island De las Pertas, waiting for the return of them who got away only to their great misfortune, hearing no news of their captain nor companions, at last embarked on the ship of a certain pirate, who happened to pass that way. This fellow came from Jamaica, with intent to land at Gracias a Dios, and from thence to enter the river with his canoes, and take the city of Carthagena. These two crews of pirates being now joined, were infinitely glad at the presence and society of one another. Those, because they found themselves delivered from their miseries, poverty, and necessities, wherein they had lived ten entire months. These, because they were now considerably strengthened, to effect with greater satisfaction their designs. Hereupon, as soon as they were arrived at Gracias a Dios, they all put themselves into canoes, and entered the river, being five hundred men, leaving only five or six persons in each ship to keep them. They took no provisions, being persuaded they should find everywhere sufficient; but these their hopes were found totally vain, not being grounded on Almighty God; for He ordained it so, that the Indians, aware of their coming, all fled, not leaving in their houses or plantations, which for the most part border on the sides of rivers, any necessary provisions or victuals: hereby, in a few days after they had quitted their ships, they were reduced to most extreme necessity and hunger; but their hopes of making their fortunes very soon, animating them for the present, they contented themselves with a few green herbs, such as they could gather on the banks of the river.

Yet all this courage and vigour lasted but a fortnight, when their hearts, as well as bodies, began to fail for hunger; insomuch as they were forced to quit the river, and betake themselves to the woods, seeking out some villages where they might find relief, but all in vain; for having ranged up and down the woods for some days, without finding the least comfort, they were forced to return to the river, where being come, they thought convenient to descend to the sea-coast where they had left their ships, not having been able to find what they sought for. In this laborious journey they were reduced to such extremity, that many of them devoured their own shoes, the sheaths of their swords, knives, and other such things, being almost ravenous, and eager to meet some Indians, intending to sacrifice them to their teeth. At last they arrived at the sea-coast, where they found some comfort and relief to their former miseries, and also means to seek more: yet the greatest part perished through faintness and other diseases contracted by hunger, which also caused the remaining part to disperse, till at last, by degrees, many or most of them fell into the same pit that Lolonois did; of whom, and of whose companions, having given a compendious narrative, I shall continue with the actions and exploits of Captain Henry Morgan, who may deservedly be called the second Lolonois, not being unlike or inferior to him, either in achievements against the Spaniards, or in robberies of many innocent people.

Chapter IX

The origin and descent of Captain Henry Morgan—His exploits, and the most remarkable actions of his life.

CAPTAIN HENRY MORGAN was born in Great Britain, in the principality of Wales; his father was a rich yeoman, or farmer, of good quality, even as most who bear that name in Wales are known to be. Morgan, when young, had no inclination to the calling of his father, and therefore left his country, and came towards the sea-coasts to seek some other employment more suitable to his aspiring humour; where he found several ships at anchor, bound for Barbadoes. With these he resolved to go in the service of one, who, according to the practice of those parts, sold him as soon as he came ashore. He served his time at Barbadoes, and obtaining his liberty, betook himself to Jamaica, there to seek new fortunes: here he found two vessels of pirates ready to go to sea; and being destitute of employment, he went with them, with intent to follow the exercises of that sort of people: he soon learned their manner of living, so exactly, that having performed three or four voyages with profit and success, he agreed with some of his comrades, who had got by the same voyages a little money, to join stocks, and buy a ship. The vessel being bought, they unanimously chose him captain and commander.

With this ship he set forth from Jamaica to cruise on the coasts of Campechy, in which voyage he took several ships, with which he returned triumphant. Here he found an old pirate, named Mansvelt (whom we have already mentioned), busied in equipping a considerable fleet, with design to land on the continent, and pillage whatever he could. Mansvelt seeing Captain Morgan return with so many prizes, judged him to be a man of courage, and chose him for his vice-admiral in that expedition: thus having fitted out fifteen ships, great and small, they sailed from Jamaica with five hundred men, Walloons and French. This fleet arrived, not long after, at the isle of St. Catherine, near the continent of Costa Rica, latitude 12 deg. 30 min. and distant thirty-five leagues from the river Chagre. Here they made their first descent, landing most of their men, who soon forced the garrison that kept the island to surrender all the forts and castles thereof; which they instantly demolished, except one, wherein they placed a hundred men of their own party, and all the slaves they had taken from the Spaniards: with the rest of their men they marched to another small island, so near St. Catherine's, that with a bridge they made in a few days, they passed thither, taking with them all the ordnance they had taken on the great island. Having ruined with fire and sword both the islands, leaving necessary orders at the said castle, they put to sea again, with their Spanish prisoners; yet these they set ashore not long after, on the firm land, near Puerto Velo: then they cruised on Costa Rica, till they came to the river Colla, designing to pillage all the towns in those parts, thence to pass to the village of Nata, to do the same.

The governor of Panama, on advice of their arrival, and of the hostilities they committed, thought it his duty to meet them with a body of men. His coming caused the pirates to retire suddenly, seeing the whole country was alarmed, and that their designs were known, and consequently defeated at that time. Hereupon, they returned to St. Catherine's, to visit the hundred men they left in garrison there. The governor of these men was a Frenchman, named Le Sieur Simon, who behaved himself very well in that charge, while Mansvelt was absent, having put the great island in a very good posture of defence, and the little one he had caused to be cultivated with many fertile plantations, sufficient to revictual the whole fleet, not only for the present, but also for a new voyage. Mansvelt was very much bent to keep the two islands in perpetual possession, being very commodiously situated for the pirates; being so near the Spanish dominions, and easily defended.

Hereupon, Mansvelt determined to return to Jamaica, to send recruits to St. Catherine's, that in case of an invasion the pirates might be provided for a defence. As soon as he arrived, he propounded his intentions to the governor there, who rejected his propositions, fearing to displease his master, the king of England; besides, that giving him the men he desired, and necessaries, he must of necessity diminish the forces of that island, whereof he was governor. Hereupon, Mansvelt, knowing that of himself he could not compass his designs, he went to Tortuga; but there, before he could put in execution what was intended, death surprised him, and put a period to his wicked life, leaving all things in suspense till the occasion I shall hereafter relate.

Le Sieur Simon, governor of St. Catherine's, receiving no news from Mansvelt, his admiral, was impatiently desirous to know the cause thereof: meanwhile, Don John Perez de Guzman, being newly come to the government of Costa Rica, thought it not convenient for the interest of Spain for that island to be in the hands of the pirates: hereupon, he equipped a considerable fleet, which he sent to retake it; but before he used violence, he writ a letter to Le Sieur Simon, telling him, that if he would surrender the island to his Catholic Majesty, he should be very well rewarded; but, in case of refusal, severely punished, when he had forced him to do it. Le Sieur Simon, seeing no probability of being able to defend it alone, nor any emolument that by so doing could accrue either to him, or his people, after some small resistance delivered it up to its true lord and master, under the same articles they had obtained it from the Spaniards; a few days after which surrender, there arrived from Jamaica an English ship, which the governor there had sent underhand, with a good supply of people, both men and women: the Spaniards from the castle having espied the ship, put forth English colours, and persuaded Le Sieur Simon to go aboard, and conduct the ship into a port they assigned him. This he performed and they were all made prisoners. A certain Spanish engineer has published in print an exact relation of the retaking of this isle by the Spaniards, which I have thought fit to insert here:—

A true relation, and particular account of the victory obtained by the arms of his Catholic Majesty against the English pirates, by the direction and valour of Don John Perez de Guzman, knight of the order of St. James, governor and captain-general of Terra Firma, and the Province of Veraguas.

The kingdom of Terra Firma, which of itself is sufficiently strong to repel and destroy great fleets, especially the pirates of Jamaica, had several ways notice imparted to the governor thereof, that fourteen English vessels cruised on the coasts belonging to his Catholic Majesty. July 14, 1665, news came to Panama, that they were arrived at Puerto de Naos, and had forced the Spanish garrison of the isle of St. Catherine, whose governor was Don Estevan del Campo, and possessed themselves of the said island, taking prisoners the inhabitants, and destroying all that they met. About the same time, Don John Perez de Guzman received particular information of these robberies from some Spaniards who escaped out of the island (and whom he ordered to be conveyed to Puerto Velo), that the said pirates came into the island May 2, by night, without being perceived; and that the next day, after some skirmishes, they took the fortresses, and made prisoners all the inhabitants and soldiers that could not escape. Upon this, Don John called a council of war, wherein he declared the great progress the said pirates had made in the dominions of his Catholic Majesty; and propounded "that it was absolutely necessary to send some forces to the isle of St. Catherine, sufficient to retake it from the pirates, the honour and interest of his Majesty of Spain being very narrowly concerned herein; otherwise the pirates by such conquests might easily, in course of time, possess themselves of all the countries thereabouts." To this some made answer, "that the pirates, not being able to subsist in the said island, would of necessity consume and waste themselves, and be forced to quit it, without any necessity of retaking it: that consequently it was not worth the while to engage in so many expenses and troubles as this would cost." Notwithstanding which, Don John being an expert and valiant soldier, ordered that provisions should be conveyed to Puerto Velo for the use of the militia, and transported himself thither, with no small danger of his life. Here he arrived July 2, with most things necessary to the expedition in hand, where he found in the port a good ship, and well mounted, called the St. Vincent, that belonged to the company of the negroes, which he manned and victualled very well, and sent to the isle of St. Catherine, constituting Captain Joseph Sanchez Ximenez, major of Puerto Velo, commander thereof. He carried with him two hundred and seventy soldiers, and thirty-seven prisoners of the same island, besides thirty-four Spaniards of the garrison of Puerto Velo, twenty-nine mulattoes of Panama, twelve Indians, very dextrous at shooting with bows and arrows, seven expert and able gunners, two lieutenants, two pilots, one surgeon, and one priest, of the order of St. Francis, for their chaplain.

Don John soon after gave orders to all the officers how to behave themselves, telling them that the governor of Carthagena would supply them with more men, boats, and all things else, necessary for that enterprise; to which effect he had already written to the said governor. July 24, Don John setting sail with a fair wind, he called before him all his people, and made them a speech, encouraging them to fight against the enemies of their country and religion, and especially against those inhuman pirates, who had committed so many horrid cruelties upon the subjects of his Catholic Majesty; withal, promising every one most liberal rewards, especially to such as should behave themselves well in the service of their king and country. Thus Don John bid them farewell, and the ship set sail under a favourable gale. The 22nd they arrived at Carthagena, and presented a letter to the governor thereof, from the noble and valiant Don John, who received it with testimonies of great affection to the person of Don John, and his Majesty's service: and seeing their resolution to be comfortable to his desires, he promised them his assistance, with one frigate, one galleon, one boat, and one hundred and twenty-six men; one half out of his own garrison, and the other half mulattoes. Thus being well provided with necessaries, they left the port of Carthagena, August 2, and the 10th they arrived in sight of St. Catherine's towards the western point thereof; and though the wind was contrary, yet they reached the port, and anchored within it, having lost one of their boats by foul weather, at the rock called Quita Signos.

The pirates, seeing our ships come to an anchor, gave them presently three guns with bullets, which were soon answered in the same coin. Hereupon, Major Joseph Sanchez Ximenez sent ashore to the pirates one of his officers to require them, in the name of the Catholic King his master, to surrender the island, seeing they had taken it in the midst of peace between the two crowns of Spain and England; and that if they would be obstinate, he would certainly put them all to the sword. The pirates made answer, that the island had once before belonged unto the government and dominions of the king of England, and that instead of surrendering it, they preferred to lose their lives.

On Friday the 13th, three negroes, from the enemy, came swimming aboard our admiral; these brought intelligence that all the pirates upon the island were only seventy-two in number, and that they were under a great consternation, seeing such considerable forces come against them. With this intelligence, the Spaniards resolved to land, and advance towards the fortresses, which ceased not to fire as many great guns against them as they possibly could; which were answered in the same manner on our side, till dark night. On Sunday, the 15th, the day of the Assumption of our Lady, the weather being very calm and clear, the Spaniards began to advance thus: The ship St. Vincent, riding admiral, discharged two whole broadsides on the battery called the Conception; the ship St. Peter, that was vice-admiral, discharged likewise her guns against the other battery named St. James: meanwhile, our people landed in small boats, directing their course towards the point of the battery last mentioned, and thence they marched towards the gate called Cortadura. Lieutenant Francis de Cazeres, being desirous to view the strength of the enemy, with only fifteen men, was compelled to retreat in haste, by reason of the great guns, which played so furiously on the place where he stood; they shooting, not only pieces of iron, and small bullets, but also the organs of the church, discharging in every shot threescore pipes at a time.

Notwithstanding this heat of the enemy, Captain Don Joseph Ramirez de Leyva, with sixty men, made a strong attack, wherein they fought on both sides very desperately, till at last he overcame, and forced the pirates to surrender the fort.

On the other side, Captain John Galeno, with ninety men, passed over the hills, to advance that way towards the castle of St. Teresa. Meanwhile Major Don Joseph Sanchez Ximenes, as commander-in-chief, with the rest of his men, set forth from the battery of St. James, passing the port with four boats, and landing, in despite of the enemy. About this same time, Captain John Galeno began to advance with the men he led to the forementioned fortress; so that our men made three attacks on three several sides, at one and the same time, with great courage; till the pirates seeing many of their men already killed, and that they could in no manner subsist any longer, retreated towards Cortadura, where they surrendered, themselves and the whole island, into our hands. Our people possessed themselves of all, and set up the Spanish colours, as soon as they had rendered thanks to God Almighty for the victory obtained on such a signalized day. The number of dead were six men of the enemies, with many wounded, and seventy prisoners: on our side was only one man killed, and four wounded.

There were found on the island eight hundred pounds of powder, two hundred and fifty pounds of small bullets, with many other military provisions. Among the prisoners were taken also, two Spaniards, who had bore arms under the English against his Catholic Majesty: these were shot to death the next day, by order of the major. The 10th day of September arrived at the isle an English vessel, which being seen at a great distance by the major, he ordered Le Sieur Simon, who was a Frenchman, to go and visit the said ship, and tell them that were on board, that the island belonged still to the English. He performed the command, and found in the said ship only fourteen men, one woman and her daughter, who were all instantly made prisoners.

The English pirates were all transported to Puerto Velo, excepting three, who by order of the governor were carried to Panama, there to work in the castle of St. Jerom. This fortification is an excellent piece of workmanship, and very strong, being raised in the middle of the port of a quadrangular form, and of very hard stone: its height is eighty-eight geometrical feet, the wall being fourteen, and the curtains seventy-five feet diameter. It was built at the expense of several private persons, the governor of the city furnishing the greatest part of the money; so that it cost his Majesty nothing.

Chapter X

Of the Island of Cuba—Captain Morgan attempts to preserve the Isle of St. Catherine as a refuge to the nest of pirates, but fails of his design—He arrives at and takes the village of El Puerto del Principe.

CAPTAIN MORGAN seeing his predecessor and admiral Mansvelt were dead, used all the means that were possible, to keep in possession the isle of St. Catherine, seated near Cuba. His chief intent was to make it a refuge and sanctuary to the pirates of those parts, putting it in a condition of being a convenient receptacle of their preys and robberies. To this effect he left no stone unmoved, writing to several merchants in Virginia and New England, persuading them to send him provisions and necessaries, towards putting the said island in such a posture of defence, as to fear no danger of invasion from any side. But all this proved ineffectual, by the Spaniards retaking the said island: yet Captain Morgan retained his courage, which put him on new designs. First, he equipped a ship, in order to gather a fleet as great, and as strong as he could. By degrees he effected it, and gave orders to every member of his fleet to meet at a certain port of Cuba, there determining to call a council, and deliberate what was best to be done, and what place first to fall upon. Leaving these preparations in this condition, I shall give my reader some small account of the said isle of Cuba, in whose port this expedition was hatched, seeing I omitted to do it in its proper place.

Cuba lies from east to west, in north latitude, from 20 to 23 deg. in length one hundred and fifty German leagues, and about forty in breadth. Its fertility is equal to that of Hispaniola; besides which, it affords many things proper for trading and commerce; such as hides of several beasts, particularly those that in Europe are called hides of Havanna. On all sides it is surrounded with many small islands, called the Cayos: these little islands the pirates use as ports of refuge. Here they have their meetings, and hold their councils, how best to assault the Spaniards. It is watered on all sides with plentiful and pleasant rivers, whose entries form both secure and spacious ports; beside many other harbours for ships, which along the calm shores and coasts adorn this rich and beautiful island; all which contribute much to its happiness, by facilitating trade, whereto they invited both natives and aliens. The chief of these ports are San Jago, Byame, Santa Maria, Espiritu Santo, Trinidad, Zagoa, Cabo de Corientes, and others, on the south side of the island: on the north side are, La Havanna, Puerto Mariano, Santa Cruz, Mata Ricos, and Barracoa.

This island hath two chief cities, to which all the towns and villages thereof give obedience. The first is Santa Jago, or St. James, seated on the south side, and having under its jurisdiction one half of the island. The chief magistrates hereof are a bishop and a governor, who command the villages and towns of the said half. The chief of these are, on the south side, Espiritu Santo, Puerto del Principe, and Bayame. On the north it has Barracoa, and De los Cayos. The greatest part of the commerce driven here comes from the Canaries, whither they transport much tobacco, sugar, and hides, which sort of merchandise are drawn to the head city from the subordinate towns and villages. Formerly the city of Santa Jago was miserably sacked by the pirates of Jamaica and Tortuga, though it is defended by a considerable castle.

The city and port De la Havanna lies between the north and west side of the island: this is one of the strongest places of the West Indies; its jurisdiction extends over the other half of the island; the chief places under it being Santa Cruz on the north side, and La Trinidad on the south. Hence is transported huge quantities of tobacco, which is sent to New Spain and Costa Rica, even as far as the South Sea, besides many ships laden with this commodity, that are consigned to Spain and other parts of Europe, not only in the leaf, but in rolls. This city is defended by three castles, very great and strong, two of which lie towards the port, and the other is seated on a hill that commands the town. It is esteemed to contain about ten thousand families. The merchants of this place trade in New Spain, Campechy, Honduras, and Florida. All ships that come from the parts before mentioned, as also from Caraccas, Carthagena and Costa Rica, are necessitated to take their provisions in at Havanna to make their voyage for Spain; this being the necessary and straight course they must steer for the south of Europe, and other parts. The plate-fleet of Spain, which the Spaniards call Flota, being homeward bound, touches here yearly to complete their cargo with hides, tobacco, and Campechy wood.

Captain Morgan had been but two months in these ports of the south of Cuba, when he had got together a fleet of twelve sail, between ships and great boats, with seven hundred fighting men, part English and part French. They called a council, and some advised to assault the city of Havanna in the night, which they said might easily be done, if they could but take any of the ecclesiastics; yea, that the city might be sacked before the castles could put themselves in a posture of defence. Others propounded, according to their several opinions, other attempts; but the former proposal was rejected, because many of the pirates, who had been prisoners at other times in the said city, affirmed nothing of consequence could be done with less than one thousand five hundred men. Moreover, that with all these people, they ought first go to the island De los Pinos, and land them in small boats about Matamona, fourteen leagues from the said city, whereby to accomplish their designs.

Finally, they saw no possibility of gathering so great a fleet, and hereupon, with what they had, they concluded to attempt some other place. Among the rest, one propounded they should assault the town of El Puerto del Principe. This proposition he persuaded to, by saying he knew that place very well, and that being at a distance from sea, it never was sacked by any pirates, whereby the inhabitants were rich, exercising their trade by ready money, with those of Havanna who kept here an established commerce, chiefly in hides. This proposal was presently admitted by Captain Morgan, and the chief of his companions. Hereupon they ordered every captain to weigh anchor and set sail, steering towards that coast nearest to El Puerto del Principe. Here is a bay named by the Spaniards El Puerto de Santa Maria: being arrived at this bay, a Spaniard, who was prisoner aboard the fleet, swam ashore by night to the town of El Puerto del Principe, giving an account to the inhabitants of the design of the pirates, which he overheard in their discourse, while they thought he did not understand English. The Spaniards upon this advice began to hide their riches, and carry away their movables; the governor immediately raised all the people of the town, freemen and slaves, and with part of them took a post by which of necessity the pirates must pass, and commanded many trees to be cut down and laid cross the ways to hinder their passage, placing several ambuscades strengthened with some pieces of cannon to play upon them on their march. He gathered in all about eight hundred men, of which detaching part into the said ambuscades, with the rest he begirt the town, drawing them up in a spacious field, whence they could see the coming of the pirates at length.

Captain Morgan, with his men, now on the march, found the avenues to the town unpassable; hereupon they took their way through the wood, traversing it with great difficulty, whereby they escaped divers ambuscades; at last they came to the plain, from its figure called by the Spaniards La Savanna, or the Sheet. The governor seeing them come, detached a troop of horse to charge them in the front, thinking to disperse them, and to pursue them with his main body: but this design succeeded not, for the pirates marched in very good order, at the sound of their drums, and with flying colours; coming near the horse they drew into a semicircle, and so advanced towards the Spaniards, who charged them valiantly for a while; but the pirates being very dextrous at their arms, and their governor, with many of their companions, being killed, they retreated towards the wood, to save themselves with more advantage; but before they could reach it, most of them were unfortunately killed by the pirates. Thus they left the victory to these new-come enemies, who had no considerable loss of men in the battle, and but very few wounded. The skirmish lasted four hours: they entered the town not without great resistance of such as were within, who defended themselves as long as possible, and many seeing the enemy in the town, shut themselves up in their own houses, and thence made several shots upon the pirates; who thereupon threatened them, saying, "If you surrender not voluntarily, you shall soon see the town in a flame, and your wives and children torn to pieces before your faces." Upon these menaces the Spaniards submitted to the discretion of the pirates, believing they could not continue there long.

As soon as the pirates had possessed themselves of the town, they enclosed all the Spaniards, men, women, children, and slaves, in several churches, and pillaged all the goods they could find; then they searched the country round about, bringing in daily many goods and prisoners, with much provision. With this they fell to making great cheer, after their old custom, without remembering the poor prisoners, whom they let starve in the churches, though they tormented them daily and inhumanly to make them confess where they had hid their goods, money, &c., though little or nothing was left them, not sparing the women and little children, giving them nothing to eat, whereby the greatest part perished.

Pillage and provisions growing scarce, they thought convenient to depart and seek new fortunes in other places; they told the prisoners, "they should find money to ransom themselves, else they should be all transported to Jamaica; and beside, if they did not pay a second ransom for the town, they would turn every house into ashes." The Spaniards hereupon nominated among themselves four fellow-prisoners to go and seek for the above-mentioned contributions; but the pirates, to the intent that they should return speedily with those ransoms, tormented several cruelly in their presence, before they departed. After a few days, the Spaniards returned, telling Captain Morgan, "We have ran up and down, and searched all the neighbouring woods and places we most suspected, and yet have not been able to find any of our own party, nor consequently any fruit of our embassy; but if you are pleased to have a little longer patience with us, we shall certainly cause all that you demand to be paid within fifteen days;" which Captain Morgan granted. But not long after, there came into the town seven or eight pirates who had been ranging in the woods and fields, and got considerable booty. These brought amongst other prisoners, a negro, whom they had taken with letters. Captain Morgan having perused them, found that they were from the governor of Santa Jago, being written to some of the prisoners, wherein he told them, "they should not make too much haste to pay any ransom for their town or persons, or any other pretext; but on the contrary, they should put off the pirates as well as they could with excuses and delays, expecting to be relieved by him in a short time, when he would certainly come to their aid." Upon this intelligence Captain Morgan immediately ordered all their plunder to be carried aboard; and withal, he told the Spaniards, that the very next day they should pay their ransoms, for he would not wait a moment longer, but reduce the whole town to ashes, if they failed of the sum he demanded.

With this intimation, Captain Morgan made no mention to the Spaniards of the letters he had intercepted. They answered, "that it was impossible for them to give such a sum of money in so short a space of time, seeing their fellow-townsmen were not to be found in all the country thereabouts." Captain Morgan knew full well their intentions, but thought it not convenient to stay there any longer, demanding of them only five hundred oxen or cows, with sufficient salt to powder them, with this condition, that they should carry them on board his ships. Thus he departed with all his men, taking with him only six of the principal prisoners as pledges. Next day the Spaniards brought the cattle and salt to the ships, and required the prisoners; but Captain Morgan refused to deliver them, till they had helped his men to kill and salt the beeves: this was performed in great haste, he not caring to stay there any longer, lest he should be surprised by the forces that were gathering against him; and having received all on board his vessels, he set at liberty the hostages. Meanwhile there happened some dissensions between the English and the French: the occasion was as follows: A Frenchman being employed in killing and salting the beeves, an English pirate took away the marrow-bones he had taken out of the ox, which these people esteem much; hereupon they challenged one another: being come to the place of duel, the Englishman stabbed the Frenchman in the back, whereby he fell down dead. The other Frenchmen, desirous of revenge, made an insurrection against the English; but Captain Morgan soon appeased them, by putting the criminal in chains to be carried to Jamaica, promising he would see justice done upon him; for though he might challenge his adversary, yet it was not lawful to kill him treacherously, as he did.

All things being ready, and on board, and the prisoners set at liberty, they sailed thence to a certain island, where Captain Morgan intended to make a dividend of what they had purchased in that voyage; where being arrived, they found nigh the value of fifty thousand pieces of eight in money and goods; the sum being known, it caused a general grief to see such a small purchase, not sufficient to pay their debts at Jamaica. Hereupon Captain Morgan proposed they should think on some other enterprise and pillage before they're turned. But the French not being able to agree with the English, left Captain Morgan with those of his own nation, notwithstanding all the persuasions he used to reduce them to continue in his company. Thus they parted with all external signs of friendship, Captain Morgan reiterating his promises to them that he would see justice done on that criminal. This he performed; for being arrived at Jamaica, he caused him to be hanged, which was all the satisfaction the French pirates could expect.

Chapter XI

Captain Morgan resolving to attack and plunder the city of Puerto Bello, equips a fleet, and with little expense and small forces takes it.

SOME may think that the French having deserted Captain Morgan, the English alone could not have sufficient courage to attempt such great actions as before. But Captain Morgan, who always communicated vigour with his words, infused such spirit into his men, as put them instantly upon new designs; they being all persuaded that the sole execution of his orders would be a certain means of obtaining great riches, which so influenced their minds, that with inimitable courage they all resolved to follow him, as did also a certain pirate of Campechy, who on this occasion joined with Captain Morgan, to seek new fortunes under his conduct. Thus Captain Morgan in a few days gathered a fleet of nine sail, either ships or great boats, wherein he had four hundred and sixty military men.

All things being ready, they put forth to sea, Captain Morgan imparting his design to nobody at present; he only told them on several occasions, that he doubted not to make a good fortune by that voyage, if strange occurrences happened not. They steered towards the continent, where they arrived in a few days near Costa Rica, all their fleet safe. No sooner had they discovered land but Captain Morgan declared his intentions to the captains, and presently after to the company. He told them he intended to plunder Puerto Bello by night, being resolved to put the whole city to the sack: and to encourage them he added, this enterprise could not fail, seeing he had kept it secret, without revealing it to anybody, whereby they could not have notice of his coming. To this proposition some answered, "they had not a sufficient number of men to assault so strong and great a city." But Captain Morgan replied, "If our number is small, our hearts are great; and the fewer persons we are, the more union and better shares we shall have in the spoil." Hereupon, being stimulated with the hope of those vast riches they promised themselves from their success, they unanimously agreed to that design. Now, that my reader may better comprehend the boldness of this exploit, it may be necessary to say something beforehand of the city of Puerto Bello.

This city is in the province of Costa Rica, 10 deg. north latitude, fourteen leagues from the gulf of Darien, and eight westwards from the port called Nombre de Dios. It is judged the strongest place the king of Spain possesses in all the West Indies, except Havanna and Carthagena. Here are two castles almost impregnable, that defend the city, situate at the entry of the port, so that no ship or boat can pass without permission. The garrison consists of three hundred soldiers, and the town is inhabited by about four hundred families. The merchants dwell not here, but only reside awhile, when the galleons come from or go for Spain, by reason of the unhealthiness of the air, occasioned by vapours from the mountains; so that though their chief warehouses are at Puerto Bello, their habitations are at Panama, whence they bring the plate upon mules, when the fair begins, and when the ships belonging to the company of negroes arrive to sell slaves.

Captain Morgan, who knew very well all the avenues of this city and the neighbouring coasts, arrived in the dusk of the evening at Puerto de Naos, ten leagues to the west of Puerto Bello. Being come hither, they sailed up the river to another harbour called Puerto Pontin, where they anchored: here they put themselves into boats and canoes, leaving in the ships only a few men to bring them next day to the port. About midnight they came to a place called Estera longa Lemos, where they all went on shore, and marched by land to the first posts of the city: they had in their company an Englishman, formerly a prisoner in those parts, who now served them for a guide: to him and three or four more they gave commission to take the sentinel, if possible, or kill him on the place: but they seized him so cunningly, as he had no time to give warning with his musket, or make any noise, and brought him, with his hands bound, to Captain Morgan, who asked him how things went in the city, and what forces they had; with other circumstances he desired to know. After every question they made him a thousand menaces to kill him, if he declared not the truth. Then they advanced to the city, carrying the said sentinel bound before them: having marched about a quarter of a league, they came to the castle near the city, which presently they closely surrounded, so that no person could get either in or out.

Being posted under the walls of the castle, Captain Morgan commanded the sentinel, whom they had taken prisoner, to speak to those within, charging them to surrender to his discretion; otherwise they should all be cut in pieces, without quarter. But they regarding none of these threats, began instantly to fire, which alarmed the city; yet notwithstanding, though the governor and soldiers of the said castle made as great resistance as could be, they were forced to surrender. Having taken the castle, they resolved to be as good as their words, putting the Spaniards to the sword, thereby to strike a terror into the rest of the city. Whereupon, having shut up all the soldiers and officers as prisoners into one room, they set fire to the powder (whereof they found great quantity) and blew up the castle into the air, with all the Spaniards that were within. This done, they pursued the course of their victory, falling upon the city, which, as yet, was not ready to receive them. Many of the inhabitants cast their precious jewels and money into wells and cisterns, or hid them in places underground, to avoid, as much as possible, being totally robbed. One of the party of pirates, assigned to this purpose, ran immediately to the cloisters, and took as many religious men and women as they could find. The governor of the city, not being able to rally the citizens, through their great confusion, retired to one of the castles remaining, and thence fired incessantly at the pirates: but these were not in the least negligent either to assault him, or defend themselves, so that amidst the horror of the assault, they made very few shots in vain; for aiming with great dexterity at the mouths of the guns, the Spaniards were certain to lose one or two men every time they charged each gun anew.

This continued very furious from break of day till noon; yea, about this time of the day the case was very dubious which party should conquer, or be conquered. At last, the pirates perceiving they had lost many men, and yet advanced but little towards gaining either this, or the other castles, made use of fire-balls, which they threw with their hands, designing to burn the doors of the castles; but the Spaniards from the walls let fall great quantities of stones, and earthen pots full of powder, and other combustible matter, which forced them to desist. Captain Morgan seeing this generous defence made by the Spaniards, began to despair of success. Hereupon, many faint and calm meditations came into his mind; neither could he determine which way to turn himself in that strait. Being thus puzzled, he was suddenly animated to continue the assault, by seeing English colours put forth at one of the lesser castles, then entered by his men; of whom he presently after spied a troop coming to meet him, proclaiming victory with loud shouts of joy. This instantly put him on new resolutions of taking the rest of the castles, especially seeing the chiefest citizens were fled to them, and had conveyed thither great part of their riches, with all the plate belonging to the churches and divine service.

To this effect, he ordered ten or twelve ladders to be made in all haste, so broad, that three or four men at once might ascend them: these being finished, he commanded all the religious men and women, whom he had taken prisoners, to fix them against the walls of the castle. This he had before threatened the governor to do, if he delivered not the castle: but his answer was, "he would never surrender himself alive." Captain Morgan was persuaded the governor would not employ his utmost force, seeing the religious women, and ecclesiastical persons, exposed in the front of the soldiers to the greatest danger. Thus the ladders, as I have said, were put into the hands of religious persons of both sexes, and these were forced, at the head of the companies, to raise and apply them to the walls: but Captain Morgan was fully deceived in his judgment of this design; for the governor, who acted like a brave soldier in performance of his duty, used his utmost endeavour to destroy whosoever came near the walls. The religious men and women ceased not to cry to him, and beg of him, by all the saints of heaven, to deliver the castle, and spare both his and their own lives; but nothing could prevail with his obstinacy and fierceness. Thus many of the religious men and nuns were killed before they could fix the ladders; which at last being done, though with great loss of the said religious people, the pirates mounted them in great numbers, and with not less valour, having fire-balls in their hands, and earthen pots full of powder; all which things, being now at the top of the walls, they kindled and cast in among the Spaniards.

This effort of the pirates was very great, insomuch that the Spaniards could no longer resist nor defend the castle, which was now entered. Hereupon they all threw down their arms, and craved quarter for their lives; only the governor of the city would crave no mercy, but killed many of the pirates with his own hands, and not a few of his own soldiers; because they did not stand to their arms. And though the pirates asked him if he would have quarter; yet he constantly answered, "By no means, I had rather die as a valiant soldier, than be hanged as a coward." They endeavoured as much as they could to take him prisoner, but he defended himself so obstinately, that they were forced to kill him, notwithstanding all the cries and tears of his own wife and daughter, who begged him, on their knees, to demand quarter, and save his life. When the pirates had possessed themselves of the castle, which was about night, they enclosed therein all the prisoners, placing the women and men by themselves, with some guards: the wounded were put in an apartment by itself, that their own complaints might be the cure of their diseases; for no other was afforded them.

This done, they fell to eating and drinking, as usual; that is, committing in both all manner of debauchery and excess, so that fifty courageous men might easily have retaken the city, and killed all the pirates. Next day, having plundered all they could find, they examined some of the prisoners (who had been persuaded by their companions to say they were the richest of the town), charging them severely to discover where they had hid their riches and goods. Not being able to extort anything from them, they not being the right persons, it was resolved to torture them: this they did so cruelly, that many of them died on the rack, or presently after. Now the president of Panama being advertised of the pillage and ruin of Puerto Bello, he employed all his care and industry to raise forces to pursue and cast out the pirates thence; but these cared little for his preparations, having their ships at hand, and determining to fire the city, and retreat. They had now been at Puerto Bello fifteen days, in which time they had lost many of their men, both by the unhealthiness of the country, and their extravagant debaucheries.

Hereupon, they prepared to depart, carrying on board all the pillage they had got, having first provided the fleet with sufficient victuals for the voyage. While these things were doing, Captain Morgan demanded of the prisoners a ransom for the city, or else he would burn it down, and blow up all the castles; withal, he commanded them to send speedily two persons, to procure the sum, which was 100,000 pieces of eight. To this effect two men were sent to the president of Panama, who gave him an account of all. The president, having now a body of men ready, set forth towards Puerto Bello, to encounter the pirates before their retreat; but, they, hearing of his coming, instead of flying away, went out to meet him at a narrow passage, which he must pass: here they placed a hundred men, very well armed, which at the first encounter put to flight a good party of those of Panama. This obliged the president to retire for that time, not being yet in a posture of strength to proceed farther. Presently after, he sent a message to Captain Morgan, to tell him, "that if he departed not suddenly with all his forces from Puerto Bello, he ought to expect no quarter for himself, nor his companions, when he should take them, as he hoped soon to do." Captain Morgan, who feared not his threats, knowing he had a secure retreat in his ships, which were at hand, answered, "he would not deliver the castles, before he had received the contribution money he had demanded; which if it were not paid down, he would certainly burn the whole city, and then leave it, demolishing beforehand the castles, and killing the prisoners."

The governor of Panama perceived by this answer that no means would serve to mollify the hearts of the pirates, nor reduce them to reason: hereupon, he determined to leave them, as also those of the city whom he came to relieve, involved in the difficulties of making the best agreement they could. Thus in a few days more the miserable citizens gathered the contributions required, and brought 100,000 pieces of eight to the pirates for a ransom of their cruel captivity: but the president of Panama was much amazed to consider that four hundred men could take such a great city, with so many strong castles, especially having no ordnance, wherewith to raise batteries, and, what was more, knowing the citizens of Puerto Bello had always great repute of being good soldiers themselves, and who never wanted courage in their own defence. This astonishment was so great, as made him send to Captain Morgan, desiring some small pattern of those arms wherewith he had taken with much vigour so great a city. Captain Morgan received this messenger very kindly, and with great civility; and gave him a pistol, and a few small bullets, to carry back to the president his master; telling him, withal, "he desired him to accept that slender pattern of the arms wherewith he had taken Puerto Bello, and keep them for a twelvemonth; after which time he promised to come to Panama, and fetch them away." The governor returned the present very soon to Captain Morgan, giving him thanks for the favour of lending him such weapons as he needed not; and, withal, sent him a ring of gold, with this message, "that he desired him not to give himself the labour of coming to Panama, as he had done to Puerto Bello: for he did assure him, he should not speed so well here, as he had done there."

After this, Captain Morgan (having provided his fleet with all necessaries, and taken with him the best guns of the castles, nailing up the rest) set sail from Puerto Bello with all his ships, and arriving in a few days at Cuba, he sought out a place wherein he might quickly make the dividend of their spoil. They found in ready money 250,000 pieces of eight, besides other merchandises; as cloth, linen, silks, &c. With this rich purchase they sailed thence to their common place of rendezvous, Jamaica. Being arrived, they passed here some time in all sorts of vices and debaucheries, according to their custom; spending very prodigally what others had gained with no small labour and toil.

Chapter XII

Captain Morgan takes the city of Maracaibo on the coast of Neuva Venezuela—Piracies committed in those seas—Ruin of three Spanish ships, set forth to hinder the robberies of the pirates.

NOT long after their arrival at Jamaica, being that short time they needed to lavish away all the riches above mentioned, they concluded on another enterprise to seek new fortunes: to this effect Captain Morgan ordered all the commanders of his ships to meet at De la Vacca, or the Cow Isle, south of Hispaniola, as is said. Hither flocked to them great numbers of other pirates, French and English; the name of Captain Morgan being now famous in all the neighbouring countries for his great enterprises. There was then at Jamaica an English ship newly come from New England, well mounted with thirty-six guns: this vessel, by order of the governor of Jamaica, joined Captain Morgan to strengthen his fleet, and give him greater courage to attempt mighty things. With this supply Captain Morgan judged himself sufficiently strong; but there being in the same place another great vessel of twenty-four iron guns, and twelve brass ones, belonging to the French, Captain Morgan endeavoured also to join this ship to his own; but the French not daring to trust the English, denied absolutely to consent.

The French pirates belonging to this great ship had met at sea an English vessel; and being under great want of victuals, they had taken some provisions out of the English ship, without paying for them, having, perhaps, no ready money aboard: only they gave them bills of exchange for Jamaica and Tortuga, to receive money there. Captain Morgan having notice of this, and perceiving he could not prevail with the French captain to follow him, resolved to lay hold on this occasion, to ruin the French, and seek his revenge. Hereupon he invited, with dissimulation, the French commander, and several of his men, to dine with him on board the great ship that was come to Jamaica, as is said. Being come, he made them all prisoners, pretending the injury aforesaid done to the English vessel.

This unjust action of Captain Morgan was soon followed by Divine punishment, as we may conceive: the manner I shall instantly relate. Captain Morgan, presently after he had taken these French prisoners, called a council to deliberate what place they should first pitch upon in this new expedition. Here it was determined to go to the isle of Savona, to wait for the flota then expected from Spain, and take any of the Spanish vessels straggling from the rest. This resolution being taken, they began aboard the great ship to feast one another for joy of their new voyage, and happy council, as they hoped: they drank many healths, and discharged many guns, the common sign of mirth among seamen. Most of the men being drunk, by what accident is not known, the ship suddenly was blown up, with three hundred and fifty Englishmen, besides the French prisoners in the hold; of all which there escaped but thirty men, who were in the great cabin, at some distance from the main force of the powder. Many more, it is thought, might have escaped, had they not been so much overtaken with wine.

This loss brought much consternation of mind upon the English; they knew not whom to blame, but at last the accusation was laid on the French prisoners, whom they suspected to have fired the powder of the ship out of revenge, though with the loss of their own lives: hereupon they added new accusations to their former, whereby to seize the ship and all that was in it, by saying the French designed to commit piracy on the English. The grounds of this accusation were given by a commission from the governor of Barracoa, found aboard the French vessel, wherein were these words, "that the said governor did permit the French to trade in all Spanish ports," &c. "As also to cruise on the English pirates in what place soever they could find them, because of the multitudes of hostilities which they had committed against the subjects of his Catholic Majesty in time of peace betwixt the two crowns." This commission for trade was interpreted as an express order to exercise piracy and war against them, though it was only a bare licence for coming into the Spanish ports; the cloak of which permission were those words, "that they should cruise upon the English." And though the French did sufficiently expound the true sense of it, yet they could not clear themselves to Captain Morgan nor his council: but in lieu thereof, the ship and men were seized and sent to Jamaica. Here they also endeavoured to obtain justice, and the restitution of their ship, but all in vain; for instead of justice, they were long detained in prison, and threatened with hanging.

Eight days after the loss of the said ship, Captain Morgan commanded the bodies of the miserable wretches who were blown up to be searched for, as they floated on the sea; not to afford them Christian burial, but for their clothes and attire: and if any had gold rings on their fingers, these were cut off, leaving them exposed to the voracity of the monsters of the sea. At last they set sail for Savona, the place of their assignation. There were in all fifteen vessels, Captain Morgan commanding the biggest, of only fourteen small guns; his number of men was nine hundred and sixty. Few days after, they arrived at the Cabo de Lobos, south of Hispaniola, between Cape Tiburon and Cape Punta de Espada: hence they could not pass by reason of contrary winds for three weeks, notwithstanding all the utmost endeavours Captain Morgan used to get forth; then they doubled the cape, and spied an English vessel at a distance. Having spoken with her, they found she came from England, and bought of her, for ready money, some provisions they wanted.

Captain Morgan proceeded on his voyage till he came to the port of Ocoa; here he landed some men, sending them into the woods to seek water and provisions, the better to spare such as he had already on board. They killed many beasts, and among others some horses. But the Spaniards, not well satisfied at their hunting, laid a stratagem for them, ordering three or four hundred men to come from Santo Domingo not far distant, and desiring them to hunt in all the parts thereabout near the sea, that so, if the pirates should return, they might find no subsistence. Within few days the same pirates returned to hunt, but finding nothing to kill, a party of about fifty straggled farther on into the woods. The Spaniards, who watched all their motions, gathered a great herd of cows, and set two or three men to keep them. The pirates having spied them, killed a sufficient number; and though the Spaniards could see them at a distance, yet they could not hinder them at present; but as soon as they attempted to carry them away, they set upon them furiously, crying, "Mata, mata," i.e., "Kill, kill." Thus the pirates were compelled to quit the prey, and retreat to their ships; but they did it in good order, retiring by degrees, and when they had opportunity, discharging full volleys on the Spaniards, killing many of their enemies, though with some loss.

The Spaniards seeing their damage, endeavoured to save themselves by flight, and carry off their dead and wounded companions. The pirates perceiving them flee, would not content themselves with what hurt they had already done, but pursued them speedily into the woods, and killed the greatest part of those that remained. Next day Captain Morgan, extremely offended at what had passed, went himself with two hundred men into the woods to seek for the rest of the Spaniards, but finding nobody, he revenged his wrath on the houses of the poor and miserable rustics that inhabit those scattering fields and woods, of which he burnt a great number: with this he returned to his ships, somewhat more satisfied in his mind for having done some considerable damage to the enemy; which was always his most ardent desire.

The impatience wherewith Captain Morgan had waited a long while for some of his ships not yet arrived, made him resolve to sail away without them, and steer for Savona, the place he always designed. Being arrived, and not finding any of his ships come, he was more impatient and concerned than before, fearing their loss, or that he must proceed without them; but he waiting for their arrival a few days longer, and having no great plenty of provisions, he sent a crew of one hundred and fifty men to Hispaniola to pillage some towns near Santo Domingo; but the Spaniards, upon intelligence of their coming, were so vigilant, and in such good posture of defence, that the pirates thought not convenient to assault them, choosing rather to return empty-handed to Captain Morgan, than to perish in that desperate enterprise.

At last Captain Morgan, seeing the other ships did not come, made a review of his people, and found only about five hundred men; the ships wanting were seven, he having only eight in his company, of which the greatest part were very small. Having hitherto resolved to cruise on the coasts of Caraccas, and to plunder the towns and villages there, finding himself at present with such small forces, he changed his resolution by advice of a French captain in his fleet. This Frenchman having served Lolonois in the like enterprises, and at the taking of Maracaibo, knew all the entries, passages, forces, and means, how to put in execution the same again in company of Captain Morgan; to whom having made a full relation of all, he concluded to sack it the second time, being himself persuaded, with all his men, of the facility the Frenchman propounded. Hereupon they weighed anchor, and steered towards Curasao. Being come within sight of it, they landed at another island near it, called Ruba, about twelve leagues from Curasao to the west. This island, defended by a slender garrison, is inhabited by Indians subject to Spain, and speak Spanish, by reason of the Roman Catholic religion, here cultivated by a few priests sent from the neighbouring continent.

The inhabitants exercise commerce or trade with the pirates that go or come this way: they buy of the islanders sheep, lambs, and kids, which they exchange for linen, thread, and like things. The country is very dry and barren, the whole substance thereof consisting in those three things, and in a little indifferent wheat. This isle produces many venomous insects, as vipers, spiders, and others. These last are so pernicious, that a man bitten by them dies mad; and the manner of recovering such is to tie them very fast both hands and feet, and so to leave them twenty-four hours, without eating or drinking anything. Captain Morgan, as was said, having cast anchor before this island, bought of the inhabitants sheep, lambs, and wood, for all his fleet. After two days, he sailed again in the night, to the intent they might not see what course he steered.

Next day they arrived at the sea of Maracaibo, taking great care not to be seen from Vigilia, for which reason they anchored out of sight of it. Night being come, they set sail again towards the land, and next morning, by break of day, were got directly over against the bar of the said lake. The Spaniards had built another fort since the action of Lolonois, whence they now fired continually against the pirates, while they put their men into boats to land. The dispute continued very hot, being managed with great courage from morning till dark night. This being come, Captain Morgan, in the obscurity thereof, drew nigh the fort, which having examined, he found nobody in it, the Spaniards having deserted it not long before. They left behind them a match lighted near a train of powder, to have blown up the pirates and the whole fortress as soon as they were in it. This design had taken effect, had not the pirates discovered it in a quarter of an hour; but Captain Morgan snatching away the match, saved both his own and his companions' lives. They found here much powder, whereof he provided his fleet, and then demolished part of the walls, nailing sixteen pieces of ordnance, from twelve to twenty-four pounders. Here they also found many muskets and other military provisions.

Next day they commanded the ships to enter the bar, among which they divided the powder, muskets, and other things found in the fort: then they embarked again to continue their course towards Maracaibo; but the waters being very low, they could not pass a certain bank at the entry of the lake: hereupon they were compelled to go into canoes and small boats, with which they arrived next day before Maracaibo, having no other defence than some small pieces which they could carry in the said boats. Being landed, they ran immediately to the fort De la Barra, which they found as the precedent, without any person in it, for all were fled into the woods, leaving also the town without any people, unless a few miserable folks, who had nothing to lose.

As soon as they had entered the town, the pirates searched every corner, to see if they could find any people that were hid, who might offend them unawares; not finding anybody, every party, as they came out of their several ships, chose what houses they pleased. The church was deputed for the common corps du guard, where they lived after their military manner, very insolently. Next day after they sent a troop of a hundred men to seek for the inhabitants and their goods; these returned next day, bringing with them thirty persons, men, women, and children, and fifty mules laden with good merchandise. All these miserable people were put to the rack, to make them confess where the rest of the inhabitants were, and their goods. Among other tortures, one was to stretch their limbs with cords, and then to beat them with sticks and other instruments. Others had burning matches placed betwixt their fingers, which were thus burnt alive. Others had slender cords or matches twisted about their heads, till their eyes burst out. Thus all inhuman cruelties were executed on those innocent people. Those who would not confess, or who had nothing to declare, died under the hands of those villains. These tortures and racks continued for three whole weeks, in which time they sent out daily parties to seek for more people to torment and rob, they never returning without booty and new riches.

Captain Morgan having now gotten into his hands about a hundred of the chief families, with all their goods, at last resolved for Gibraltar, as Lolonois had done before: with this design he equipped his fleet, providing it sufficiently with all necessaries. He put likewise on board all the prisoners, and weighing anchor, set sail with resolution to hazard a battle. They had sent before some prisoners to Gibraltar, to require the inhabitants to surrender, otherwise Captain Morgan would certainly put them all to the sword, without any quarter. Arriving before Gibraltar, the inhabitants received him with continual shooting of great cannon bullets; but the pirates, instead of fainting hereat, ceased not to encourage one another, saying, "We must make one meal upon bitter things, before we come to taste the sweetness of the sugar this place affords."

Next day very early they landed all their men, and being guided by the Frenchman abovesaid, they marched towards the town, not by the common way, but crossing through the woods, which way the Spaniards scarce thought they would have come; for at the beginning of their march they made as if they intended to come the next and open way to the town, hereby to deceive the Spaniards: but these remembering full well what Lolonois had done but two years before, thought it not safe to expect a second brunt, and hereupon all fled out of the town as fast as they could, carrying all their goods and riches, as also all the powder; and having nailed all the great guns, so as the pirates found not one person in the whole city, but one poor innocent man who was born a fool. This man they asked whither the inhabitants were fled, and where they had hid their goods. To all which questions and the like, he constantly answered, "I know nothing, I know nothing:" but they presently put him to the rack, and tortured him with cords; which torments forced him to cry out, "Do not torture me any more, but come with me, and I will show you my goods and my riches." They were persuaded, it seems, he was some rich person disguised under those clothes so poor, and that innocent tongue; so they went along with him, and he conducted them to a poor miserable cottage, wherein he had a few earthen dishes and other things of no value, and three pieces of eight, concealed with some other trumpery underground. Then they asked him his name, and he readily answered, "My name is Don Sebastian Sanchez, and I am brother unto the governor of Maracaibo." This foolish answer, it must be conceived, these inhuman wretches took for truth: for no sooner had they heard it, but they put him again upon the rack, lifting him up on high with cords, and tying huge weights to his feet and neck. Besides which, they burnt him alive, applying palm-leaves burning to his face.

The same day they sent out a party to seek for the inhabitants, on whom they might exercise their cruelties. These brought back an honest peasant with two daughters of his, whom they intended to torture as they used others, if they showed not the places where the inhabitants were hid. The peasant knew some of those places, and seeing himself threatened with the rack, went with the pirates to show them; but the Spaniards perceiving their enemies to range everywhere up and down the woods, were already fled thence farther off into the thickest of the woods, where they built themselves huts, to preserve from the weather those few goods they had. The pirates judged themselves deceived by the peasant, and hereupon, to revenge themselves, notwithstanding all his excuses and supplication, they hanged him on a tree.

Then they divided into parties to search the plantations; for they knew the Spaniards that were absconded could not live on what the woods afforded, without coming now and then for provisions to their country houses. Here they found a slave, to whom they promised mountains of gold and his liberty, by transporting him to Jamaica, if he would show them where the inhabitants of Gibraltar lay hid. This fellow conducted them to a party of Spaniards, whom they instantly made prisoners, commanding this slave to kill some before the eyes of the rest; that by this perpetrated crime, he might never be able to leave their wicked company. The negro, according to their orders, committed many murders and insolencies upon the Spaniards, and followed the unfortunate traces of the pirates; who eight days after returned to Gibraltar with many prisoners, and some mules laden with riches. They examined every prisoner by himself (who were in all about two hundred and fifty persons), where they had hid the rest of their goods, and if they know of their fellow-townsmen. Such as would not confess were tormented after a most inhuman manner. Among the rest, there happened to be a Portuguese, who by a negro was reported, though falsely, to be very rich; this man was commanded to produce his riches. His answer was, he had no more than one hundred pieces of eight in the world, and these had been stolen from him two days before by his servant; which words, though he sealed with many oaths and protestations, yet they would not believe him, but dragging him to the rack, without any regard to his age of sixty years, they stretched him with cords, breaking both his arms behind his shoulders.

This cruelty went not alone; for he not being able or willing to make any other declaration, they put him to another sort of torment more barbarous; they tied him with small cords by his two thumbs and great toes to four stakes fixed in the ground, at a convenient distance, the whole weight of his body hanging on those cords. Not satisfied yet with this cruel torture, they took a stone of above two hundred pounds, and laid it upon his belly, as if they intended to press him to death; they also kindled palm leaves, and applied the flame to the face of this unfortunate Portuguese, burning with them the whole skin, beard, and hair. At last, seeing that neither with these tortures, nor others, they could get anything out of him, they untied the cords, and carried him half dead to the church, where was their corps du guard; here they tied him anew to one of the pillars thereof, leaving him in that condition, without giving him either to eat or drink, unless very sparingly, and so little that would scarce sustain life for some days; four or five being past, he desired one of the prisoners might come to him, by whose means he promised he would endeavour to raise some money to satisfy their demands. The prisoner whom he required was brought to him, and he ordered him to promise the pirate five hundred pieces of eight for his ransom; but they were deaf and obstinate at such a small sum, and instead of accepting it, beat him cruelly with cudgels, saying, "Old fellow, instead of five hundred, you must say five hundred thousand pieces of eight; otherwise you shall here end your life." Finally, after a thousand protestations that he was but a miserable man, and kept a poor tavern for his living, he agreed with them for one thousand pieces of eight. These he raised, and having paid them, got his liberty; though so horribly maimed, that it is scarce to be believed he could survive many weeks.

Others were crucified by these tyrants, and with kindled matches burnt between the joints of their fingers and toes: others had their feet put into the fire, and thus were left to be roasted alive. Having used these and other cruelties with the white men, they began to practise the same with the negroes, their slaves, who were treated with no less inhumanity than their masters.

Among these slaves was one who promised Captain Morgan to conduct him to a river of the lake, where he should find a ship and four boats, richly laden with goods of the inhabitants of Maracaibo: the same discovered likewise where the governor of Gibraltar lay hid, with the greatest part of the women of the town; but all this he revealed, upon great menaces to hang him, if he told not what he knew. Captain Morgan sent away presently two hundred men in two settees, or great boats, to this river, to seek for what the slave had discovered; but he himself, with two hundred and fifty more, undertook to go and take the governor. This gentleman was retired to a small island in the middle of the river, where he had built a little fort, as well as he could, for his defence; but hearing that Captain Morgan came in person with great forces to seek him, he retired to the top of a mountain not far off, to which there was no ascent but by a very narrow passage, so straight, that whosoever did attempt to gain the ascent, must march his men one by one. Captain Morgan spent two days before he arrived at this little island, whence he designed to proceed to the mountain where the governor was posted, had he not been told of the impossibility of ascent, not only for the narrowness of the way, but because the governor was well provided with all sorts of ammunition: beside, there was fallen a huge rain, whereby all the pirates' baggage and powder was wet. By this rain, also, they lost many men at the passage over a river that was overflown: here perished, likewise, some women and children, and many mules laden with plate and goods, which they had taken from the fugitive inhabitants; so that things were in a very bad condition with Captain Morgan, and his men much harassed, as may be inferred from this relation: whereby, if the Spaniards, in that juncture, had had but fifty men well armed, they might have entirely destroyed the pirates. But the fears the Spaniards had at first conceived were so great, that the leaves stirring on the trees they often fancied to be pirates. Finally, Captain Morgan and his people, having upon this march sometimes waded up to their middles in water for half, or whole miles together, they at last escaped, for the greatest part; but the women and children for the major part died.

Thus twelve days after they set forth to seek the governor they returned to Gibraltar, with many prisoners: two days after arrived also the two settees that went to the river, bringing with them four boats, and some prisoners; but the greatest part of the merchandise in the said boats they found not, the Spaniards having unladed and secured it, having intelligence of their coming; who designed also, when the merchandise was taken out, to burn the boats: yet the Spaniards made not so much haste to unlade these vessels, but that they left in the ship and boats great parcels of goods, which the pirates seized, and brought a considerable booty to Gibraltar. Thus, after they had been in possession of the place five entire weeks, and committed an infinite number of murders, robberies, and such-like insolencies, they concluded to depart; but first they ordered some prisoners to go forth into the woods and fields, and collect a ransom for the town, otherwise they would certainly burn it down to the ground. These poor afflicted men went as they were sent, and having searched the adjoining fields and woods, returned to Captain Morgan, telling him they had scarce been able to find anybody, but that to such as they had found they had proposed his demands; to which they had answered, that the governor had prohibited them to give any ransom for the town, but they beseeched him to have a little patience, and among themselves they would collect five thousand pieces of eight; and for the rest, they would give some of their own townsmen as hostages, whom he might carry to Maracaibo, till he had received full satisfaction.

Captain Morgan having now been long absent from Maracaibo, and knowing the Spaniards had had sufficient time to fortify themselves, and hinder his departure out of the lake, granted their proposition, and made as much haste as he could for his departure: he gave liberty to all the prisoners, first putting every one to a ransom; yet he detained the slaves. They delivered him four persons agreed on for hostages of what money more he was to receive, and they desired to have the slave mentioned above, intending to punish him according to his deserts; but Captain Morgan would not deliver him, lest they should burn him alive. At last, they weighed anchor, and set sail in all haste for Maracaibo: here they arrived in four days, and found all things as they had left them; yet here they received news from a poor distressed old man, whom alone they found sick in the town, that three Spanish men-of-war were arrived at the entry of the lake, waiting the return of the pirates: moreover, that the castle at the entry thereof was again put into a good posture of defence, well provided with guns and men, and all sorts of ammunition.

This relation could not choose but disturb the mind of Captain Morgan, who now was careful how to get away through the narrow entry of the lake: hereupon he sent his swiftest boat to view the entry, and see if things were as they had been related. Next day the boat came back, confirming what was said; assuring him, they had viewed the ships so nigh, that they had been in great danger of their shot, hereunto they added, that the biggest ship was mounted with forty guns, the second with thirty, and the smallest with twenty-four. These forces being much beyond those of Captain Morgan, caused a general consternation in the pirates, whose biggest vessel had not above fourteen small guns. Every one judged Captain Morgan to despond, and to be hopeless, considering the difficulty of passing safe with his little fleet amidst those great ships and the fort, or he must perish. How to escape any other way, by sea or land, they saw no way. Under these necessities, Captain Morgan resumed new courage, and resolving to show himself still undaunted, he boldly sent a Spaniard to the admiral of those three ships, demanding of him a considerable ransom for not putting the city of Maracaibo to the flames. This man (who was received by the Spaniards with great admiration of the boldness of those pirates) returned two days after, bringing to Captain Morgan a letter from the said admiral, as follows:—

The Letter of Don Alonso del Campo y Espinosa, Admiral of the Spanish Fleet, to Captain Morgan, Commander of the Pirates.

"Having understood by all our friends and neighbours, the unexpected news that you have dared to attempt and commit hostilities in the countries, cities, towns, and villages belonging to the dominions of his Catholic Majesty, my sovereign lord and master; I let you understand by these lines, that I am come to this place, according to my obligation, near that castle which you took out of the hands of a parcel of cowards; where I have put things into a very good posture of defence, and mounted again the artillery which you had nailed and dismounted. My intent is, to dispute with you your passage out of the lake, and follow and pursue you everywhere, to the end you may see the performance of my duty. Notwithstanding, if you be contented to surrender with humility all that you have taken, together with the slaves and all other prisoners, I will let you freely pass, without trouble or molestation; on condition that you retire home presently to your own country. But if you make any resistance or opposition to what I offer you, I assure you I will command boats to come from Caraccas, wherein I will put my troops, and coming to Maracaibo, will put you every man to the sword. This is my last and absolute resolution. Be prudent, therefore, and do not abuse my bounty with ingratitude. I have with me very good soldiers, who desire nothing more ardently than to revenge on you, and your people, all the cruelties, and base infamous actions, you have committed upon the Spanish nation in America. Dated on board the royal ship named the Magdalen, lying at anchor at the entry of the lake of Maracaibo, this 24th of April, 1669.

"Don Alonso del Campo y Espinosa."

As soon as Captain Morgan received this letter, he called all his men together in the market-place of Maracaibo, and after reading the contents thereof, both in French and English, asked their advice and resolution on the whole matter, and whether they had rather surrender all they had got to obtain their liberty, than fight for it.

They answered all, unanimously, they had rather fight to the last drop of blood, than surrender so easily the booty they had got with so much danger of their lives. Among the rest, one said to Captain Morgan, "Take you care for the rest, and I will undertake to destroy the biggest of those ships with only twelve men: the manner shall be, by making a brulot, or fire-ship, of that vessel we took in the river of Gibraltar; which, to the intent she may not be known for a fireship, we will fill her decks with logs of wood, standing with hats and montera caps, to deceive their sight with the representation of men.

The same we will do at the port-holes that serve for the guns, which shall be filled with counterfeit cannon. At the stern we will hang out English colours, and persuade the enemy she is one of our best men-of-war going to fight them." This proposition was admitted and approved by every one; howbeit, their fears were not quite dispersed.

For, notwithstanding what had been concluded there, they endeavoured the next day to come to an accommodation with Don Alonso. To this effect, Captain Morgan sent to him two persons, with these propositions: First, that he would quit Maracaibo, without doing any damage to the town, or exacting any ransom for the firing thereof. Secondly, that he would set at liberty one half of the slaves, and all the prisoners, without ransom. Thirdly, that he would send home freely the four chief inhabitants of Gibraltar, which he had in his custody as hostages for the contributions those people had promised to pay. These propositions were instantly rejected by Don Alonso, as dishonourable: neither would he hear of any other accommodation, but sent back this message: "That if they surrendered not themselves voluntarily into his hands, within two days, under the conditions which he had offered them by his letter, he would immediately come, and force them to do it."

No sooner had Captain Morgan received this message from Don Alonso, than he put all things in order to fight, resolving to get out of the lake by main force, without surrendering anything. First, he commanded all the slaves and prisoners to be tied, and guarded very well, and gathered all the pitch, tar, and brimstone, they could find in the whole town, for the fire-ship above-mentioned; then they made several inventions of powder and brimstone with palm leaves, well annointed with tar. They covered very well their counterfeit cannon, laying under every piece many pounds of powder; besides, they cut down many outworks of the ship, that the powder might exert its strength the better; breaking open, also, new port-holes, where, instead of guns, they placed little drums used by the negroes. Finally, the decks were handsomely beset with many pieces of wood, dressed up like men with hats, or monteras, and armed with swords, muskets, and bandeleers.

The fire-ship being thus fitted, they prepared to go to the entry of the port. All the prisoners were put into one great boat, and in another of the biggest they placed all the women, plate, jewels, and other rich things: into others they put the bales of goods and merchandise, and other things of bulk: each of these boats had twelve men aboard, very well armed; the brulot had orders to go before the rest of the vessels, and presently to fall foul with the great ship. All things being ready, Captain Morgan exacted an oath of all his comrades, protesting to defend themselves to the last drop of blood, without demanding quarter; promising withal, that whosoever behaved himself thus, should be very well rewarded.

With this courageous resolution they set sail to seek the Spaniards. On April 30, 1669, they found the Spanish fleet riding at anchor in the middle of the entry of the lake. Captain Morgan, it being now late and almost dark, commanded all his vessels to an anchor, designing to fight even all night if they forced him to it. He ordered a careful watch to be kept aboard every vessel till morning, they being almost within shot, as well as within sight of the enemy. The day dawning, they weighed anchor, and sailed again, steering directly towards the Spaniards; who seeing them move, did instantly the same. The fire-ship sailing before the rest fell presently upon the great ship, and grappled her; which the Spaniards (too late) perceiving to be a fire-ship, they attempted to put her off, but in vain: for the flame seizing her timber and tackling, soon consumed all the stern, the fore part sinking into the sea, where she perished. The second Spanish ship perceiving the admiral to burn, not by accident, but by industry of the enemy, escaped towards the castle, where the Spaniards themselves sunk her, choosing to lose their ship rather than to fall into the hands of those pirates. The third, having no opportunity to escape, was taken by the pirates. The seamen that sunk the second ship near the castle, perceiving the pirates come towards them to take what remains they could find of their shipwreck (for some part was yet above water), set fire also to this vessel, that the pirates might enjoy nothing of that spoil. The first ship being set on fire, some of the persons in her swam towards the shore; these pirates would have taken up in their boats, but they would not ask or take quarter, choosing rather to lose their lives than receive them from their hands, for reasons which I shall relate.

The pirates being extremely glad at this signal victory so soon obtained, and with so great an inequality of forces, conceived greater pride than they had before, and all presently ran ashore, intending to take the castle. This they found well provided with men, cannon, and ammunition, they having no other arms than muskets, and a few hand granadoes: their own artillery they thought incapable, for its smallness, of making any considerable breach in the walls. Thus they spent the rest of the day, firing at the garrison with their muskets, till the dusk of the evening, when they attempted to advance nearer the walls, to throw in their fire-balls: but the Spaniards resolving to sell their lives as dear as they could, fired so furiously at them, that they having experimented the obstinacy of the enemy, and seeing thirty of their men dead, and as many more wounded, they retired to their ships.

The Spaniards believing the pirates would next day renew the attack with their own cannon, laboured hard all night to put things in order for their coming; particularly, they dug down, and made plain, some little hills and eminences, when possibly the castle might be offended.

But Captain Morgan intended not to come again, busying himself next day in taking prisoners some of the men who still swam alive, hoping to get part of the riches lost in the two ships that perished. Among the rest, he took a pilot, who was a stranger, and who belonged to the lesser ship of the two, of whom he inquired several things; as, What number of people those three ships had in them? Whether they expected any more ships to come? From what port they set forth last, when they came to seek them out? He answered, in Spanish, "Noble sir, be pleased to pardon and spare me, that no evil be done to me, being a stranger to this nation I have served, and I shall sincerely inform you of all that passed till our arrival at this lake. We were sent by orders from the Supreme Council of State in Spain, being six men-of-war well equipped, into these seas, with instructions to cruise upon the English pirates, and root them out from these parts by destroying as many of them as we could.

"These orders were given, upon the news brought to the court of Spain of the loss and ruin of Puerto Bello, and other places; of all which damages and hostilities committed here by the English, dismal lamentations have often been made to the catholic king and council, to whom belongs the care and preservation of this new world. And though the Spanish court hath many times by their ambassadors complained hereof to the king of England; yet it hath been the constant answer of his Majesty of Great Britain, that he never gave any letters patent, nor commissions, for acting any hostility against the subjects of the king of Spain. Hereupon the catholic king resolved to revenge his subjects, and punish these proceedings: commanded six men-of-war to be equipped, which he sent under the command of Don Augustine de Bustos, admiral of the said fleet. He commanded the biggest ship, named N. S. de la Soleda, of forty-eight great guns, and eight small ones. The vice-admiral was Don Alonso del Campo y Espinosa, who commanded the second ship called La Conception, of forty-four great guns, and eight small ones; besides four vessels more, whereof the first was named the Magdalen, of thirty-six great guns, and twelve small ones, with two hundred and fifty men. The second was called St. Lewis, with twenty-six great guns, twelve small ones, and two hundred men. The third was called La Marquesa, of sixteen great guns, eight small ones, and one hundred and fifty men. The fourth and last, N. S. del Carmen, with eighteen great guns, eight small ones, and one hundred and fifty men.

"Being arrived at Carthagena, the two greatest ships received orders to return to Spain, being judged too big for cruising on these coasts. With the four ships remaining, Don Alonso del Campo y Espinosa departed towards

Campechy to seek the English: we arrived at the port there, where, being surprised by a huge storm from the north, we lost one of our ships, being that which I named last. Hence we sailed for Hispaniola, in sight of which we came in a few days, and steered for Santo Domingo: here we heard that there had passed that way a fleet from Jamaica, and that some men thereof had landed at Alta Gracia; the inhabitants had taken one prisoner, who confessed their design was to go and pillage the city of Caraccas. On this news, Don Alonso instantly weighed anchor, and, crossing over to the continent, we came in sight of the Caraccas: here we found them not, but met with a boat, which certified us they were in the lake of Maracaibo, and that the fleet consisted of seven small ships, and one boat.

"Upon this we came here, and arriving at the entry of the lake, we shot off a gun for a pilot from the shore. Those on land perceiving we were Spaniards, came willingly to us with a pilot, and told us the English had taken Maracaibo, and that they were now at the pillage of Gibraltar. Don Alonso, on this news, made a handsome speech to his soldiers and mariners, encouraging them to their duty, and promising to divide among them all they should take from the English: he ordered the guns we had taken out of the ship that was lost to be put into the castle, and mounted for its defence, with two eighteen-pounders more, out of his own ship. The pilots conducted us into the port, and Don Alonso commanded the people on shore to come before him, whom he ordered to repossess the castle, and reinforce it with one hundred men more than it had before its being taken. Soon after, we heard of your return from Gibraltar to Maracaibo, whither Don Alonso wrote you a letter, giving you an account of his arrival and design, and exhorting you to restore what you had taken. This you refusing, he renewed his promises to his soldiers and seamen, and having given a very good supper to all his people, he ordered them not to take or give any quarter, which was the occasion of so many being drowned, who dared not to crave quarter, knowing themselves must give none. Two days before you came against us, a negro came aboard Don Alonso's ship, telling him, 'Sir, be pleased to have great care of yourself; for the English have prepared a fire-ship, with design to burn your fleet.' But Don Alonso not believing this, answered, 'How can that be? Have they, peradventure, wit enough to build a fire-ship? Or what instruments have they to do it withal?'"

This pilot having related so distinctly these things to Captain Morgan, was very well used by him, and, after some kind proffers made to him, remained in his service. He told Captain Morgan, that, in the ship which was sunk, there was a great quantity of plate, to the value of forty thousand pieces of eight; which occasioned the Spaniards to be often seen in boats about it. Hereupon, Captain Morgan ordered one of his ships to remain there, to find ways of getting out of it what plate they could; meanwhile, himself, with all his fleet, returned to Maracaibo, where he refitted the great ship he had taken, and chose it for himself, giving his own bottom to one of his captains.

Then he sent again a messenger to the admiral, who was escaped ashore, and got into the castle, demanding of him a ransom of fire for Maracaibo; which being denied, he threatened entirely to consume and destroy it. The Spaniards considering the ill-luck they had all along with those pirates, and not knowing how to get rid of them, concluded to pay the said ransom, though Don Alonso would not consent.

Hereupon, they sent to Captain Morgan, to know what sum he demanded. He answered, that on payment of 30,000 pieces of eight, and five hundred beeves, he would release the prisoners and do no damage to the town. At last they agreed on 20,000 pieces of eight, and five hundred beeves to victual his fleet. The cattle were brought the next day, with one part of the money; and, while the pirates were busied in salting the flesh, they made up the whole 20,000 pieces of eight, as was agreed.

But Captain Morgan would not presently deliver the prisoners, as he had promised, fearing the shot of the castle at his going forth out of the lake. Hereupon he told them he intended not to deliver them till he was out of that danger, hoping thus to obtain a free passage. Then he set sail with his fleet in quest of the ship he had left, to seek for the plate of the vessel that was burnt. He found her on the place, with 15,000 pieces of eight got out of the work, beside many pieces of plate, as hilts of swords, and the like; also a great quantity of pieces of eight melted and run together, by the force of the fire.

Captain Morgan scarce thought himself secure, nor could he contrive how to avoid the shot of the castle: hereupon he wished the prisoners to agree with the governor to permit a safe passage to his fleet, which, if he should not allow, he would certainly hang them all up in his ships. Upon this the prisoners met, and appointed some of their fellow-messengers to go to the said governor, Don Alonso: these went to him, beseeching and supplicating him to have compassion on those afflicted prisoners, who were, with their wives and children, in the hands of Captain Morgan; and that to this effect he would be pleased to give his word to let the fleet of pirates freely pass, this being the only way to save both the lives of them that came with this petition, as also of those who remained in captivity; all being equally menaced with the sword and gallows, if he granted them not this humble request. But Don Alonso gave them for answer a sharp reprehension of their cowardice, telling them, "If you had been as loyal to your king in hindering the entry of these pirates, as I shall do their going out, you had never caused these troubles, neither to yourselves nor to our whole nation, which hath suffered so much through your pusillanimity. In a word, I shall never grant

91

your request, but shall endeavour to maintain that respect which is due to my king, according to my duty."

Thus the Spaniards returned with much consternation, and no hopes of obtaining their request, telling Captain Morgan what answer they had received: his reply was, "If Don Alonso will not let me pass, I will find means how to do it without him." Hereupon he presently made a dividend of all they had taken, fearing he might not have an opportunity to do it in another place, if any tempest should rise and separate the ships, as also being jealous that any of the commanders might run away with the best part of the spoil, which then lay much more in one vessel than another. Thus they all brought in according to their laws, and declared what they had, first making oath not to conceal the least thing. The accounts being cast up, they found to the value of 25,000 pieces of eight, in money and jewels, beside the huge quantity of merchandise and slaves, all which purchase was divided to every ship or boat, according to her share.

The dividend being made, the question still remained how they should pass the castle, and get out of the lake. To this effect they made use of a stratagem, as follows: the day before the night wherein they determined to get forth, they embarked many of their men in canoes, and rowed towards the shore, as if they designed to land: here they hid themselves under branches of trees that hang over the coast awhile, laying themselves down in the boats; then the canoes returned to the ships, with the appearance of only two or three men rowing them back, the rest being unseen at the bottom of the canoes: thus much only could be perceived from the castle, and this false landing of men, for so we may call it, was repeated that day several times: this made the Spaniards think the pirates intended at night to force the castle by scaling it. This fear caused them to place most of their great guns on the land side, together with their main force, leaving the side towards the sea almost destitute of defence.

Night being come, they weighed anchor, and by moonlight, without setting sail, committed themselves to the ebbing tide, which gently brought them down the river, till they were near the castle; being almost over against it, they spread their sails with all possible haste. The Spaniards perceiving this, transported with all speed their guns from the other side, and began to fire very furiously at them; but these having a very favourable wind, were almost past danger before those of the castle could hurt them; so that they lost few of their men, and received no considerable damage in their ships. Being out of the reach of the guns, Captain Morgan sent a canoe to the castle with some of the prisoners, and the governor thereof gave them a boat to return to their own homes; but he detained the hostages from Gibraltar, because the rest of the ransom for not firing the place was yet unpaid. Just as he departed, Captain Morgan ordered seven great guns with bullets to be fired against the castle, as it were to take his leave of them, but they answered not so much as with a musket shot.

Next day after, they were surprised with a great tempest, which forced them to cast anchor in five or six fathom water: but the storm increasing, compelled them to weigh again, and put to sea, where they were in great danger of being lost; for if they should have been cast on shore, either into the hands of the Spaniards or Indians, they would certainly have obtained no mercy: at last, the tempest being spent, the wind ceased, to the great joy of the whole fleet.

While Captain Morgan made his fortune by these pillagings, his companions, who were separated from his fleet at the Cape de Lobos, to take the ship spoken of before, endured much misery, and were unfortunate in all their attempts. Being arrived at Savona, they found not Captain Morgan there, nor any of their companions, nor had they the fortune to find a letter which Captain Morgan at his departure left behind him in a place where in all probability they would meet with it. Thus, not knowing what course to steer, they concluded to pillage some town or other. They were in all about four hundred men, divided into four ships and one boat: being ready to set forth, they constituted an admiral among themselves, being one who had behaved himself very courageously at the taking of Puerto Bello, named Captain Hansel. This commander attempted the taking of the town of Commana, on the continent of Caraccas, nigh sixty leagues to the west of the Isle de la Trinidad. Being arrived there, they landed their men, and killed some few Indians near the coast; but approaching the town, the Spaniards having in their company many Indians, disputed the entry so briskly, that, with great loss and confusion, they were forced to retire to the ships. At last they arrived at Jamaica, where the rest of their companions, who came with Captain Morgan, mocked and jeered them for their ill success at Commana, often telling them, "Let us see what money you brought from Commana, and if it be as good silver as that which we bring from Maracaibo."

Chapter XIII

Captain Morgan goes to Hispaniola to equip a new fleet, with intent to pillage again on the coast of the West Indies.

CAPTAIN MORGAN perceived now that Fortune favoured him, by giving success to all his enterprises, which occasioned him, as is usual in human affairs, to aspire to greater things, trusting she would always be constant to him.

Such was the burning of Panama, wherein Fortune failed not to assist him, as she had done before, though she had led him thereto through a thousand difficulties. The history hereof I shall now relate, being so remarkable in all its circumstances, as peradventure nothing more deserving memory will be read by future ages.

Captain Morgan arriving at Jamaica, found many of his officers and soldiers reduced to their former indigency, by their vices and debaucheries. Hence they perpetually importuned him for new exploits.

Captain Morgan, willing to follow Fortune's call, stopped the mouths of many inhabitants of Jamaica, who were creditors to his men for large sums, with the hopes and promises of greater achievements than ever, by a new expedition. This done, he could easily levy men for any enterprise, his name being so famous through all those islands as that alone would readily bring him in more men than he could well employ. He undertook therefore to equip a new fleet, for which he assigned the south side of Tortuga as a place of rendezvous, writing letters to all the expert pirates there inhabiting, as also to the governor, and to the planters and hunters of Hispaniola, informing them of his intentions, and desiring their appearance, if they intended to go with him. These people upon this notice flocked to the place assigned, in huge numbers, with ships, canoes, and boats, being desirous to follow him. Many, who had not the convenience of coming by sea, traversed the woods of Hispaniola, and with no small difficulties arrived there by land. Thus all were present at the place assigned, and ready against October 24, 1670.

Captain Morgan was not wanting to be there punctually, coming in his ship to Port Couillon, over against the island De la Vaca, the place assigned. Having gathered the greatest part of his fleet, he called a council to deliberate about finding provisions for so many people. Here they concluded to send four ships and one boat, with four hundred men, to the continent, in order to rifle some country towns and villages for all the corn or maize they could gather. They set sail for the continent towards the river De la Hacha, designing to assault the village called La Rancheria, usually best stored with maize of all the parts thereabouts. Meanwhile Captain Morgan sent another party to hunt in the woods, who killed a huge number of beasts, and salted them: the rest remained in the ships, to clean, fit, and rig them, that, at the return of their fellows, all things might be in a readiness to weigh anchor and follow their designs.

Chapter XIV

What happened in the river De la Hacha.

THESE four ships setting sail from Hispaniola, steered for the river De la Hacha, where they were suddenly overtaken with a tedious calm. Being within sight of land becalmed for some days, the Spaniards inhabiting along the coast, who had perceived them to be enemies, had sufficient time to prepare themselves, at least to hide the best of their goods, that, without any care of preserving them, they might be ready to retire, if they proved unable to resist the pirates, by whose frequent attempts on those coasts they had already learned what to do in such cases. There was then in the river a good ship, come from Carthagena to lade with maize, and now almost ready to depart. The men of this ship endeavoured to escape; but, not being able to do it, both they and the vessel fell into their hands. This was a fit purchase for them, being good part of what they came for. Next morning, about break of day, they came with their ships ashore, and landed their men, though the Spaniards made good resistance from a battery they had raised on that side, where, of necessity, they were to land; but they were forced to retire to a village, whither the pirates followed them. Here the Spaniards rallying, fell upon them with great fury, and maintained a strong combat, which lasted till night; but then, perceiving they had lost a great number of men, which was no less on the pirates' side, they retired to secret places in the woods.

Next day the pirates seeing them all fled, and the town left empty of people, they pursued them as far as they could, and overtook a party of Spaniards, whom they made prisoners, and exercised with most cruel torments, to discover their goods. Some were forced, by intolerable tortures, to confess; but others, who would not, were used more barbarously. Thus, in fifteen days that they remained there, they took many prisoners, much plate and movables, with which booty they resolved to return to Hispaniola: yet, not content with what they had got, they dispatched some prisoners into the woods to seek for the rest of the inhabitants, and to demand a ransom for not burning the town. They answered, they had no money nor plate; but if they would be satisfied with a quantity of maize, they would give as much as they could. The pirates accepted this, it being then more useful to them than ready money, and agreed they should pay four thousand hanegs, or bushels of maize. These were brought in three days after, the Spaniards being desirous to rid themselves of that inhuman sort of people. Having laded them on board with the rest of their purchase, they returned to Hispaniola, to give account to their leader, Captain Morgan, of all they had performed.

They had now been absent five weeks on this commission, which long delay occasioned Captain Morgan almost in despair of their return, fearing lest they were fallen in to the hands of the Spaniards; especially considering the place whereto they went could easily be relieved from Carthagena and Santa Maria, if the inhabitants were careful to alarm the country. On the other side, he feared lest they should have made some great fortune in that voyage, and with it have escaped to some other place. But seeing his ships return in greater numbers than they departed, he resumed new courage, this sight causing both in him and his companions infinite joy, especially when they found them full laden with maize, which they much wanted for the maintenance of so many people, from whom they expected great matters under such a commander.

Captain Morgan having divided the said maize, as also the flesh which the hunters brought, among his ships, according to the number of men, he concluded to depart; having viewed beforehand every ship, and observed their being well equipped and clean. Thus he set sail, and stood for Cape Tiburon, where he determined to resolve what enterprise he should take in hand. No sooner were they arrived, but they met some other ships newly come to join them from Jamaica; so that now their fleet consisted of thirty-seven ships, wherein were two thousand fighting men, beside mariners and boys. The admiral hereof was mounted with twenty-two great guns, and six small ones of brass; the rest carried some twenty; some sixteen, some eighteen, and the smallest vessel at least four; besides which, they had great quantities of ammunition and fire-balls, with other inventions of powder.

Captain Morgan having such a number of ships, divided the whole fleet into two squadrons, constituting a vice-admiral, and other officers of the second squadron, distinct from the former. To these he gave letters patent, or commissions to act all manner of hostilities against the Spanish nation, and take of them what ships they could, either abroad at sea, or in the harbours, as if they were open and declared enemies (as he termed it) of the king of England, his pretended master. This done, he called all his captains and other officers together, and caused them to sign some articles of agreement betwixt them, and in the name of all. Herein it was stipulated, that he should have the hundredth part of all that was gotten to himself: that every captain should draw the shares of eight men for the expenses of his ship, besides his own. To the surgeon, beside his pay, two hundred pieces of eight for his chest of medicaments. To every carpenter, above his salary, one hundred pieces of eight. The rewards were settled in this voyage much higher than before: as, for the loss of both legs, fifteen hundred pieces of eight, or fifteen slaves, the choice left to the party, for the loss of both hands, eighteen hundred pieces of eight, or eighteen slaves: for one leg, whether right or left, six hundred pieces of eight, or six slaves: for a hand, as much as for a leg; and for the loss of an eye, one hundred pieces of eight, or one slave. Lastly, to him that in any battle should signalize himself, either by entering first any castle, or taking down the Spanish colours, and setting up the English, they allotted fifty pieces of eight for a reward. All which extraordinary salaries and rewards to be paid out of the first spoil they should take, as every one should occur to be either rewarded or paid.

This contract being signed, Captain Morgan commanded his vice-admirals and captains to put all things in order, to attempt one of these three places; either Carthagena, Panama, or Vera Cruz. But the lot fell on Panama, as the richest of all three; though this city being situate at such a distance from the North Sea as they knew not well the approaches to it, they judged it necessary to go beforehand to the isle of St. Catherine, there to find some persons for guides in this enterprise; for in the garrison there are commonly many banditti and outlaws belonging to Panama and the neighbouring places, who are very expert in the knowledge of that country. But before they proceeded, they published an act through the whole fleet, promising, if they met with any Spanish vessel, the first captain who should take it should have for his reward the tenth part of what should be found in her.

Chapter XV

Captain Morgan leaves Hispaniola and goes to St. Catherine's, which he takes.

CAPTAIN MORGAN and his companions weighed anchor from the Cape of Tiburon, December 16, 1670. Four days after they arrived in sight of St. Catherine's, now in possession of the Spaniards again, as was said before, to which they commonly banish the malefactors of the Spanish dominions in the West Indies. Here are huge quantities of pigeons at certain seasons. It is watered by four rivulets, whereof two are always dry in summer. Here is no trade or commerce exercised by the inhabitants; neither do they plant more fruits than what are necessary for human life, though the country would make very good plantations of tobacco of considerable profit, were it cultivated.

As soon as Captain Morgan came near the island with his fleet, he sent one of his best sailing vessels to view the entry of the river, and see if any other ships were there, who might hinder him from landing; as also fearing lest they should give intelligence of his arrival to the inhabitants, and prevent his designs.

Next day, before sunrise, all the fleet anchored near the island, in a bay called Aguade Grande. On this bay the Spaniards had built a battery, mounted with four pieces of cannon. Captain Morgan landed about one thousand men in divers squadrons, marching through the woods, though they had no other guides than a few of his own men, who had been there before, under Mansvelt. The same day they came to a place where the governor sometimes resided: here they found a battery called the Platform, but nobody in it, the Spaniards having retired to the lesser island, which, as was said before, is so near the great one, that a short bridge only may conjoin them.

This lesser island was so well fortified with forts and batteries round it, as might seem impregnable. Hereupon, as soon as the Spaniards perceived the pirates approach, they fired on them so furiously, that they could advance nothing that day, but were content to retreat, and take up their rest in the open fields, which was not strange to these people, being sufficiently used to such kind of repose. What most afflicted them was hunger, having not eat anything that whole day. About midnight it rained so hard, that they had much ado to bear it, the greatest part of them having no other clothes than a pair of seaman's trousers or breeches, and a shirt, without shoes or stockings. In this great extremity they pulled down a few thatched houses to make fires withal; in a word, they were in such a condition, that one hundred men, indifferently well armed, might easily that night have torn them all in pieces. Next morning, about break of day, the rain ceased, and they dried their arms and marched on: but soon after it rained afresh, rather harder than before, as if the skies were melted into waters; which kept them from advancing towards the forts, whence the Spaniards continually fired at them.

The pirates were now reduced to great affliction and danger, through the hardness of the weather, their own nakedness, and great hunger; for a small relief hereof, they found in the fields an old horse, lean, and full of scabs and blotches, with galled back and sides: this they instantly killed and flayed, and divided in small pieces among themselves, as far as it would reach (for many could not get a morsel) which they roasted and devoured without salt or bread, more like ravenous wolves than men. The rain not ceasing, Captain Morgan perceived their minds to relent, hearing many of them say they would return on board. Among these fatigues of mind and body, he thought convenient to use some sudden remedy: to this effect, he commanded a canoe to be rigged in haste, and colours of truce to be hanged out. This canoe he sent to the Spanish governor, with this message: "That if within a few hours he delivered not himself and all his men into his hands, he did by that messenger swear to him, and all those that were in his company, he would most certainly put them to the sword, without granting quarter to any."

In the afternoon the canoe returned with this answer: "That the governor desired two hours' time to deliberate with his officers about it, which being past, he would give his positive answer." The time being elapsed, the governor sent two canoes with white colours, and two persons to treat with Captain Morgan; but, before they landed, they demanded of the pirates two persons as hostages. These were readily granted by Captain Morgan, who delivered them two of the captains for a pledge of the security required. With this the Spaniards propounded to Captain Morgan, that the governor, in a full assembly, had resolved to deliver up the island, not being provided with sufficient forces to defend it against such an armada. But withal, he desired Captain Morgan would be pleased to use a certain stratagem of war, for the better saving of his own credit, and the reputation of his officers both abroad and at home, which should be as follows:—That Captain Morgan would come with his troops by night to the bridge that joined the lesser island to the great one, and there attack the fort of St. Jerome: that at the same time all his fleet would draw near the castle of Santa Teresa, and attack it by land, landing, in the meanwhile, more troops near the battery of St. Matthew: that these troops being newly landed, should by this means intercept the governor as he endeavoured to pass to St. Jerome's fort, and then take him prisoner; using the formality, as if they forced him to deliver the castle; and that he would lead the English into it, under colour of being his own troops. That on both sides there should be continual firing, but without bullets, or at least into the air, so that no side might be hurt. That thus having obtained two such considerable forts, the chiefest of the isle, he need not take care for the rest, which must fall of course into his hands.

These propositions were granted by Captain Morgan, on condition they should see them faithfully observed; otherwise they should be used with the utmost rigour: this they promised to do, and took their leave, to give account of their negotiation to the governor. Presently after, Captain Morgan commanded the whole fleet to enter the port, and his men to be ready to assault, that night, the castle of St. Jerome. Thus the false battle began, with incessant firing from both the castles, against the ships, but without bullets, as was agreed. Then the pirates landed, and assaulted by night the lesser island, which they took, as also both fortresses; forcing the Spaniards, in appearance, to fly to the church. Before this assault, Captain Morgan sent word to the governor, that he should keep all his men together in a body; otherwise, if the pirates met any straggling Spaniards in the streets, they should certainly shoot them.

This island being taken by this unusual stratagem, and all things put in order, the pirates made a new war against the poultry, cattle, and all sorts of victuals they could find, for some days; scarce thinking of anything else than to kill, roast, and eat, and make what good cheer they could. If wood was wanting, they pulled down the houses, and made fires with the timber, as had been done before in the field. Next day they numbered all the prisoners they had taken upon the island, which were found to be in all four hundred and fifty-nine persons, men, women, and children; viz., one hundred and ninety soldiers of the garrison; forty inhabitants, who were married: forty-three children, thirty-four slaves, belonging to the king; with eight children, eight banditti, thirty-nine negroes belonging to private persons; with twenty-seven female blacks, and thirty-four children. The pirates disarmed all the Spaniards, and sent them out immediately to the plantations to seek for provisions, leaving the women in the church to exercise their devotions.

Soon after they reviewed the whole island, and all the fortresses thereof, which they found to be nine in all, viz., the fort of St. Jerome, next the bridge, had eight great guns, of twelve, six, and eight pounds carriage; with six pipes of muskets, every pipe containing ten muskets. Here they found still sixty muskets, with sufficient powder and other ammunition. The second fortress, called St. Matthew, had three guns, of eight pounds each. The third, and chiefest, named Santa Teresa, had twenty great guns, of eighteen, twelve, eight, and six pounds; with ten pipes of muskets, like those before, and ninety muskets remaining, besides other ammunition. This castle was built with stone and mortar, with very thick walls, and a large ditch round it, twenty feet deep, which, though it was dry, yet was very hard to get over. Here was no entry, but through one door, to the middle of the castle. Within it was a mount, almost inaccessible, with four pieces of cannon at the top; whence they could shoot directly into the port. On the sea side it was impregnable, by reason of the rocks round it, and the sea beating furiously upon them. To the land it was so commodiously seated on a mountain, as there was no access to it but by a path three or four feet broad. The fourth fortress was named St. Augustine, having three guns of eight and six pounds. The fifth, named La Plattaforma de la Conception, had only two guns, of eight pounds. The sixth, by name San Salvador, had likewise no more than two guns. The seventh, called Plattaforma de los Artilleros, had also two guns. The eighth, called Santa Cruz, had three guns. The ninth, called St. Joseph's Fort, had six guns, of twelve and eight pounds, besides two pipes of muskets, and sufficient ammunition.

In the storehouses were above thirty thousand pounds of powder, with all other ammunition, which was carried by the pirates on board. All the guns were stopped and nailed, and the fortresses demolished, except that of St. Jerome, where the pirates kept guard and resistance. Captain Morgan inquired for any banditti from Panama or Puerto Bello, and three were brought him, who pretended to be very expert in the avenues of those parts. He asked them to be his guides, and show him the securest ways to Panama, which, if they performed, he promised them equal shares in the plunder of that expedition, and their liberty when they arrived in Jamaica. These propositions the banditti readily accepted, promising to serve him very faithfully, especially one of the three, who was the greatest rogue, thief, and assassin among them, who had deserved rather to be broken alive on the wheel, than punished with serving in a garrison. This wicked fellow had a great ascendant over the other two, and domineered over them as he pleased, they not daring to disobey his orders.

Captain Morgan commanded four ships and one boat to be equipped, and provided with necessaries, to go and take the castle of Chagre, on the river of that name; neither would he go himself with his whole fleet, lest the Spaniards should be jealous of his farther design on Panama. In these vessels he embarked four hundred men, to put in execution these his orders. Meanwhile, himself remained in St. Catherine's with the rest of the fleet, expecting to hear of their success.

Chapter XVI

Captain Morgan takes the Castle of Chagre, with four hundred men sent to this purpose from St. Catherine's.

CAPTAIN MORGAN sending this little fleet to Chagre, chose for vice-admiral thereof one Captain Brodely, who had been long in those quarters, and committed many robberies on the Spaniards, when Mansvelt took the isle of St. Catherine, as was before related; and therefore was thought a fit person for this exploit, his actions likewise having rendered him famous among the pirates, and their enemies the Spaniards. Captain Brodely being made commander, in three days after his departure arrived in sight of the said castle of Chagre, by the Spaniards called St. Lawrence. This castle is built on a high mountain, at the entry of the river, surrounded by strong palisades, or wooden walls, filled with earth, which secures them as well as the best wall of stone or brick. The top of this mountain is, in a manner, divided into two parts, between which is a ditch thirty feet deep. The castle hath but one entry, and that by a drawbridge over this ditch. To the land it has four bastions, and to the sea two more. The south part is totally inaccessible, through the cragginess of the mountain. The north is surrounded by the river, which here is very broad. At the foot of the castle, or rather mountain, is a strong fort, with eight great guns, commanding the entry of the river. Not much lower are two other batteries, each of six pieces, to defend likewise the mouth of the river. At one side of the castle are two great storehouses of all sorts of warlike ammunition and merchandise, brought thither from the island country. Near these houses is a high pair of stairs hewn out of the rock, to mount to the top of the castle. On the west is a small port, not above seven or eight fathoms deep, fit for small vessels, and of very good anchorage; besides, before the castle, at the entry of the river, is a great rock, scarce to be described but at low tides.

No sooner had the Spaniards perceived the pirates, but they fired incessantly at them with the biggest of their guns. They came to an anchor in a small port, about a league from the castle. Next morning, very early, they went ashore, and marched through the woods, to attack the castle on that side. This march lasted till two of the clock in the afternoon, before they could reach the castle, by reason of the difficulties of the way, and its mire and dirt; and though their guides served them very exactly, yet they came so nigh the castle at first, that they lost many of their men by its shot, they being in an open place without covert. This much perplexed the pirates, not knowing what course to take; for on that side, of necessity, they must make the assault: and being uncovered from head to foot, they could not advance one step without danger: besides that, the castle, both for its situation and strength, made them much doubt of success. But to give it over they dared not, lest they should be reproached by their companions.

At last, after many doubts and disputes, resolving to hazard the assault and their lives desperately, they advanced towards the castle with their swords in one hand, and fire-balls in the other. The Spaniards defended themselves very briskly, ceasing not to fire at them continually; crying withal, "Come on, ye English dogs! enemies to God and our king; and let your other companions that are behind come on too, ye shall not go to Panama this bout." The pirates making some trial to climb the walls, were forced to retreat, resting themselves till night. This being come, they returned to the assault, to try, by the help of their fire-balls, to destroy the pales before the wall; and while they were about it, there happened a very remarkable accident, which occasioned their victory. One of the pirates being wounded with an arrow in his back, which pierced his body through, he pulled it out boldly at the side of his breast, and winding a little cotton about it, he put it into his musket, and shot it back to the castle; but the cotton being kindled by the powder, fired two or three houses in the castle, being thatched with palm-leaves, which the Spaniards perceived not so soon as was necessary; for this fire meeting with a parcel of powder, blew it up, thereby causing great ruin, and no less consternation to the Spaniards, who were not able to put a stop to it, not having seen it time enough.

The pirates perceiving the effect of the arrow, and the misfortunes of the Spaniards, were infinitely glad; and while they were busied in quenching the fire, which caused a great confusion for want of water, the pirates took this opportunity, setting fire likewise to the palisades. The fire thus seen at once in several parts about the castle, gave them great advantage against the Spaniards, many breaches being made by the fire among the pales, great heaps of earth falling into the ditch. Then the pirates climbing up, got over into the castle, though those Spaniards, who were not busy about the fire, cast down many flaming pots full of combustible matter, and odious smells, which destroyed many of the English.

The Spaniards, with all their resistance, could not hinder the palisades from being burnt down before midnight. Meanwhile the pirates continued in their intention of taking the castle; and though the fire was very great, they would creep on the ground, as near as they could, and shoot amidst the flames against the Spaniards on the other side, and thus killed many from the walls. When day was come, they observed all the movable earth, that lay betwixt the pales, to be fallen into the ditch; so that now those within the castle lay equally exposed to them without, as had been on the contrary before; whereupon the pirates continued shooting very furiously, and killed many Spaniards; for the governor had charged them to make good those posts, answering to the heaps of earth fallen into the ditch, and caused the artillery to be transported to the breaches.

The fire within the castle still continuing, the pirates from abroad did what they could to hinder its progress, by shooting incessantly against it; one party of them was employed only for this, while another watched all the motions of the Spaniards. About noon the English gained a breach, which the governor himself defended with twenty-five soldiers. Here was made a very courageous resistance by the Spaniards, with muskets, pikes, stones, and swords; but through all these the pirates fought their way, till they gained the castle. The Spaniards, who remained alive, cast themselves down from the castle into the sea, choosing rather to die thus (few or none surviving the fall) than to ask quarter for their lives. The governor himself retreated to the corps du gard, before which were placed two pieces of cannon: here he still defended himself, not demanding any quarter, till he was killed with a musket-shot in the head.

The governor being dead, and the corps du gard surrendering, they found remaining in it alive thirty men, whereof scarce ten were not wounded: these informed the pirates that eight or nine of their soldiers had deserted, and were gone to Panama, to carry news of their arrival and invasion. These thirty men alone remained of three hundred and fourteen wherewith the castle was garrisoned, among which not one officer was found alive. These were all made prisoners, and compelled to tell whatever they knew of their designs and enterprises. Among other things, that the governor of Panama had notice sent him three weeks ago from Carthagena, that the English were equipping a fleet at Hispaniola, with a design to take Panama; and, beside, that this had been discovered by a deserter from the pirates at the river De la Hacha, where they had victualled. That upon this, the governor had sent one hundred and sixty-four men to strengthen the garrison of that castle, with much provision and ammunition; the ordinary garrison whereof was only one hundred and fifty men, but these made up two hundred and fourteen men, very well armed. Besides this, they declared that the governor of Panama had placed several ambuscades along the river of Chagre; and that he waited for them in the open fields of Panama with three thousand six hundred men.

The taking of this castle cost the pirates excessively dear, in comparison to what they were wont to lose, and their toil and labour was greater than at the conquest of the isle of St. Catherine; for, numbering their men, they had lost above a hundred, beside seventy wounded. They commanded the Spanish prisoners to cast the dead bodies of their own men from the top of the mountain to the seaside, and to bury them. The wounded were carried to the church, of which they made an hospital, and where also they shut up the women.

Captain Morgan remained not long behind at St. Catherine's, after taking the castle of Chagre, of which he had notice presently; but before he departed, he embarked all the provisions that could be found, with much maize, or Indian wheat, and cazave, whereof also is made bread in those ports. He transported great store of provisions to the garrison of Chagre, whencesoever they could be got. At a certain place they cast into the sea all the guns belonging thereto, designing to return, and leave that island well garrisoned, to the perpetual possession of the pirates; but he ordered all the houses and forts to be fired, except the castle of St. Teresa, which he judged to be the strongest and securest wherein to fortify himself at his return from Panama.

Having completed his arrangements, he took with him all the prisoners of the island, and then sailed for Chagre, where he arrived in eight days. Here the joy of the whole fleet was so great, when they spied the English colours on the castle, that they minded not their way into the river, so that they lost four ships at the entry thereof, Captain Morgan's being one; yet they saved all the men and goods. The ships, too, had been preserved, if a strong northerly wind had not risen, which cast them on the rock at the entry of the river.

Captain Morgan was brought into the castle with great acclamations of all the pirates, both of those within, and those newly come. Having heard the manner of the conquest, he commanded all the prisoners to work, and repair what was necessary, especially to set up new palisades round the forts of the castle. There were still in the river some Spanish vessels, called chatten, serving for transportation of merchandise up and down the river, and to go to Puerto Bello and Nicaragua. These commonly carry two great guns of iron, and four small ones of brass. These vessels they seized, with four little ships they found there, and all the canoes. In the castle they left a garrison of five hundred men, and in the ships in the river one hundred and fifty more. This done, Captain Morgan departed for Panama at the head of twelve hundred men. He carried little provisions with him, hoping to provide himself sufficiently among the Spaniards, whom he knew to lie in ambuscade by the way.

Chapter XVII

Captain Morgan departs from Chagre, at the head of twelve hundred men, to take the city of Panama.

CAPTAIN MORGAN set forth from the castle of Chagre, towards Panama, August 18, 1670. He had with him twelve hundred men, five boats laden with artillery, and thirty-two canoes. The first day they sailed only six leagues, and came to a place called De los Bracos. Here a party of his men went ashore, only to sleep and stretch their limbs, being almost crippled with lying too much crowded in the boats. Having rested awhile, they went abroad to seek victuals in the neighbouring plantations; but they could find none, the Spaniards being fled, and carrying with them all they had. This day, being the first of their journey, they had such scarcity of victuals, as the greatest part were forced to pass with only a pipe of tobacco, without any other refreshment.

Next day, about evening, they came to a place called Cruz de Juan Gallego. Here they were compelled to leave their boats and canoes, the river being very dry for want of rain, and many trees having fallen into it.

The guides told them, that, about two leagues farther, the country would be very good to continue the journey by land. Hereupon they left one hundred and sixty men on board the boats, to defend them, that they might serve for a refuge in necessity.

Next morning, being the third day, they all went ashore, except those who were to keep the boats. To these Captain Morgan gave order, under great penalties, that no man, on any pretext whatever, should dare to leave the boats, and go ashore; fearing lest they should be surprised by an ambuscade of Spaniards in the neighbouring woods, which appeared so thick as to seem almost impenetrable. This morning beginning their march, the ways proved so bad, that Captain Morgan thought it more convenient to transport some of the men in canoes (though with great labour) to a place farther up the river, called Cedro Bueno. Thus they re-embarked, and the canoes returned for the rest; so that about night they got altogether at the said place. The pirates much desired to meet some Spaniards or Indians, hoping to fill their bellies with their provisions, being reduced to extremity and hunger.

The fourth day the greatest part of the pirates marched by land, being led by one of the guides; the rest went by water farther up, being conducted by another guide, who always went before them, to discover, on both sides the river, the ambuscades. These had also spies, who were very dextrous to give notice of all accidents, or of the arrival of the pirates, six hours, at least, before they came. This day, about noon, they came near a post called Torna Cavallos: here the guide of the canoes cried out, that he perceived an ambuscade. His voice caused infinite joy to all the pirates, hoping to find some provisions to satiate their extreme hunger. Being come to the place, they found nobody in it, the Spaniards being fled, and leaving nothing behind but a few leathern bags, all empty, and a few crumbs of bread scattered on the ground where they had eaten. Being angry at this, they pulled down a few little huts which the Spaniards had made, and fell to eating the leathern bags, to allay the ferment of their stomachs, which was now so sharp as to gnaw their very bowels. Thus they made a huge banquet upon these bags of leather, divers quarrels arising concerning the greatest shares. By the bigness of the place, they conjectured about five hundred Spaniards had been there, whom, finding no victuals, they were now infinitely desirous to meet, intending to devour some of them rather than perish.

Having feasted themselves with those pieces of leather, they marched on, till they came about night to another post, called Torna Munni. Here they found another ambuscade, but as barren as the former. They searched the neighbouring woods, but could not find anything to eat, the Spaniards having been so provident, as not to leave anywhere the least crumb of sustenance, whereby the pirates were now brought to this extremity. Here again he was happy that had reserved since noon any bit of leather to make his supper of, drinking after it a good draught of water for his comfort. Some, who never were out of their mothers' kitchens, may ask, how these pirates could eat and digest those pieces of leather, so hard and dry? Whom I answer, that, could they once experiment what hunger, or rather famine, is, they would find the way as the pirates did. For these first sliced it in pieces, then they beat it between two stones, and rubbed it, often dipping it in water, to make it supple and tender. Lastly, they scraped off the hair, and broiled it. Being thus cooked, they cut it into small morsels, and ate it, helping it down with frequent gulps of water, which, by good fortune, they had at hand.

The fifth day, about noon, they came to a place called Barbacoa. Here they found traces of another ambuscade, but the place totally as unprovided as the former. At a small distance were several plantations, which they searched very narrowly, but could not find any person, animal, or other thing, to relieve their extreme hunger. Finally, having ranged about, and searched a long time, they found a grot, which seemed to be but lately hewn out of a rock, where were two sacks of meal, wheat, and like things, with two great jars of wine, and certain fruits called platanoes. Captain Morgan, knowing some of his men were now almost dead with hunger, and fearing the same of the rest, caused what was found to be distributed among them who were in greatest necessity. Having refreshed themselves with these victuals, they marched anew with greater courage than ever. Such as were weak were put into the canoes, and those commanded to land that were in them before. Thus they prosecuted their journey till late at night; when coming to a plantation, they took up their rest, but without eating anything; for the Spaniards, as before, had swept away all manner of provisions.

The sixth day they continued their march, part by land and part by water. Howbeit, they were constrained to rest very frequently, both for the ruggedness of the way, and their extreme weakness, which they endeavoured to relieve by eating leaves of trees and green herbs, or grass; such was their miserable condition. This day at noon they arrived at a plantation, where was a barn full of maize. Immediately they beat down the doors and ate it dry, as much as they could devour; then they distributed a great quantity, giving every man a good allowance. Thus provided, and prosecuting their journey for about an hour, they came to another ambuscade. This they no sooner discovered, but they threw away their maize, with the sudden hopes of finding all things in abundance. But they were much deceived, meeting neither Indians nor victuals, nor anything else: but they saw, on the other side of the river, about a hundred Indians, who, all fleeing, escaped. Some few pirates leaped into the river to cross it, and try to take any of the Indians, but in vain: for, being much more nimble than the pirates, they not only baffled them, but killed two or three with their arrows; hooting at them, and crying, "Ha, perros! a la savana, a la savana."—"Ha, ye dogs! go to the plain, go to the plain."

This day they could advance no farther, being necessitated to pass the river, to continue their march on the other side. Hereupon they reposed for that night, though their sleep was not profound; for great murmurings were made at Captain Morgan, and his conduct; some being desirous to return home, while others would rather die there than go back a step from their undertaking: others, who had greater courage, laughed and joked at their discourses. Meanwhile, they had a guide who much comforted them, saying, "It would not now be long before they met with people from whom they should reap some considerable advantage."

The seventh day, in the morning, they made clean their arms, and every one discharged his pistol, or musket, without bullet, to try their firelocks. This done, they crossed the river, leaving the post where they had rested, called Santa Cruz, and at noon they arrived at a village called Cruz. Being yet far from the place, they perceived much smoke from the chimneys: the sight hereof gave them great joy, and hopes of finding people and plenty of good cheer. Thus they went on as fast as they could, encouraging one another, saying, "There is smoke comes out of every house: they are making good fires, to roast and boil what we are to eat;" and the like.

At length they arrived there, all sweating and panting, but found no person in the town, nor anything eatable to refresh themselves, except good fires, which they wanted not; for the Spaniards, before their departure, had every one set fire to his own house, except the king's storehouses and stables.

They had not left behind them any beast, alive or dead, which much troubled their minds, not finding anything but a few cats and dogs, which they immediately killed and devoured. At last, in the king's stables, they found, by good fortune, fifteen or sixteen jars of Peru wine, and a leathern sack full of bread. No sooner had they drank of this wine, when they fell sick, almost every man: this made them think the wine was poisoned, which caused a new consternation in the whole camp, judging themselves now to be irrecoverably lost. But the true reason was, their want of sustenance, and the manifold sorts of trash they had eaten. Their sickness was so great, as caused them to remain there till the next morning, without being able to prosecute their journey in the afternoon. This village is seated in 9 deg. 2 min. north latitude, distant from the river Chagre twenty-six Spanish leagues, and eight from Panama. This is the last place to which boats or canoes can come; for which reason they built here storehouses for all sorts of merchandise, which to and from Panama are transported on the backs of mules.

Here Captain Morgan was forced to leaves his canoes, and land all his men, though never so weak; but lest the canoes should be surprised, or take up too many men for their defence, he sent them all back to the place where the boats were, except one, which he hid, that it might serve to carry intelligence. Many of the Spaniards and Indians of this village having fled to the near plantations, Captain Morgan ordered that none should go out of the village, except companies of one hundred together, fearing lest the enemy should take an advantage upon his men. Notwithstanding, one party contravened these orders, being tempted with the desire of victuals: but they were soon glad to fly into the town again, being assaulted with great fury by some Spaniards and Indians, who carried one of them away prisoner.

Thus the vigilancy and care of Captain Morgan was not sufficient to prevent every accident.

The eighth day in the morning Captain Morgan sent two hundred men before the body of his army, to discover the way to Panama, and any ambuscades therein: the path being so narrow, that only ten or twelve persons could march abreast, and often not so many. After ten hours' march they came to a place called Quebrada Obscura: here, all on a sudden, three or four thousand arrows were shot at them, they not perceiving whence they came, or who shot them: though they presumed it was from a high rocky mountain, from one side to the other, whereon was a grot, capable of but one horse or other beast laded. This multitude of arrows much alarmed the pirates, especially because they could not discover whence they were discharged. At last, seeing no more arrows, they marched a little farther, and entered a wood: here they perceived some Indians to fly as fast as they could, to take the advantage of another post, thence to observe their march; yet there remained one troop of Indians on the place, resolved to fight and defend themselves, which they did with great courage till their captain fell down wounded; who, though he despaired of life, yet his valour being greater than his strength, would ask no quarter, but, endeavouring to raise himself, with undaunted mind laid hold of his azagayo, or javelin, and struck at one of the pirates; but before he could second the blow, he was shot to death. This was also the fate of many of his companions, who, like good soldiers, lost their lives with their captain, for the defence of their country.

The pirates endeavoured to take some of the Indians prisoners, but they being swifter than the pirates, every one escaped, leaving eight pirates dead, and ten wounded: yea, had the Indians been more dextrous in military affairs, they might have defended that passage, and not let one man pass. A little while after they came to a large champaign, open, and full of fine meadows; hence they could perceive at a distance before them some Indians, on the top of a mountain, near the way by which they were to pass: they sent fifty men, the nimblest they had, to try to catch any of them, and force them to discover their companions: but all in vain; for they escaped by their nimbleness, and presently showed themselves in another place, hallooing to the English, and crying, "A la savana, a la savana, perros Ingleses!" that is, "To the plain, to the plain, ye English dogs!" Meanwhile the ten pirates that were wounded were dressed, and plastered up.

Here was a wood, and on each side a mountain. The Indians possessed themselves of one, and the pirates of the other. Captain Morgan was persuaded the Spaniards had placed an ambuscade there, it lying so conveniently: hereupon, he sent two hundred men to search it. The Spaniards and Indians perceiving the pirates descend the mountain, did so too, as if they designed to attack them; but being got into the wood, out of sight of the pirates, they were seen no more, leaving the passage open.

About night fell a great rain, which caused the pirates to march the faster, and seek for houses to preserve their arms from being wet; but the Indians had set fire to every one, and driven away all their cattle, that the pirates, finding neither houses nor victuals, might be constrained to return: but, after diligent search, they found a few shepherds' huts, but in them nothing to eat. These not holding many men, they placed in them, out of every company, a small number, who kept the arms of the rest: those who remained in the open field endured much hardship that night, the rain not ceasing till morning.

Next morning, about break of day, being the ninth of that tedious journey, Captain Morgan marched on while the fresh air of the morning lasted; for the clouds hanging yet over their heads, were much more favourable than the scorching rays of the sun, the way being now more difficult than before. After two hours' march, they discovered about twenty Spaniards, who observed their motions: they endeavoured to catch some of them, but could not, they suddenly disappearing, and absconding themselves in caves among the rocks, unknown to the pirates. At last, ascending a high mountain, they discovered the South Sea. This happy sight, as if it were the end of their labours, caused infinite joy among them: hence they could descry also one ship, and six boats, which were set forth from Panama, and sailed towards the islands of Tavoga and Tavogilla: then they came to a vale where they found much cattle, whereof they killed good store: here, while some killed and flayed cows, horses, bulls, and chiefly asses, of which there were most; others kindled fires, and got wood to roast them: then cutting the flesh into convenient pieces, or gobbets, they threw them into the fire, and, half carbonaded or roasted, they devoured them, with incredible haste and appetite; such was their hunger, as they more resembled cannibals than Europeans; the blood many times running down from their beards to their waists.

Having satisfied their hunger, Captain Morgan ordered them to continue the march. Here, again, he sent before the main body fifty men to take some prisoners, if they could; for he was much concerned, that in nine days he could not meet one person to inform him of the condition and forces of the Spaniards. About evening they discovered about two hundred Spaniards, who hallooed to the pirates, but they understood not what they said. A little while after they came in sight of the highest steeple of Panama: this they no sooner discovered but they showed signs of extreme joy, casting up their hats into the air, leaping and shouting, just as if they had already obtained the victory, and accomplished their designs. All their trumpets sounded, and drums beat, in token of this alacrity of their minds: thus they pitched their camp for that night, with general content of the whole army, waiting with impatience for the morning, when they intended to attack the city. This evening appeared fifty horse, who came out of the city, on the noise of the drums and trumpets, to observe, as it was thought, their motions: they came almost within musket-shot of the army, with a trumpet that sounded marvellously well. Those on horseback hallooed aloud to the pirates, and threatened them, saying, "Perros! nos veremos," that is, "Ye dogs! we shall meet ye." Having made this menace, they returned to the city, except only seven or eight horsemen, who hovered thereabouts to watch their motions. Immediately after the city fired, and ceased not to play their biggest guns all night long against the camp, but with little or no harm to the pirates, whom they could not easily reach. Now also the two hundred Spaniards, whom the pirates had seen in the afternoon, appeared again, making a show of blocking up the passages, that no pirates might escape their hands: but the pirates, though in a manner besieged, instead of fearing their blockades, as soon as they had placed sentinels about their camp, opened their satchels, and, without any napkins or plates, fell to eating, very heartily, the pieces of bulls' and horses' flesh which they had reserved since noon. This done, they laid themselves down to sleep on the grass, with great repose and satisfaction, expecting only, with impatience, the dawning of the next day.

The tenth day, betimes in the morning, they put all their men in order, and, with drums and trumpets sounding, marched directly towards the city; but one of the guides desired Captain Morgan not to take the common highway, lest they should find in it many ambuscades. He took his advice, and chose another way through the wood, though very irksome and difficult. The Spaniards perceiving the pirates had taken another way they scarce had thought on, were compelled to leave their stops and batteries, and come out to meet them. The governor of Panama put his forces in order, consisting of two squadrons, four regiments of foot, and a huge number of wild bulls, which were driven by a great number of Indians, with some negroes, and others, to help them.

The pirates, now upon their march, came to the top of a little hill, whence they had a large prospect of the city and champaign country underneath. Here they discovered the forces of the people of Panama, in battle array, to be so numerous, that they were surprised with fear, much doubting the fortune of the day: yea, few or none there were but wished themselves at home, or at least free from the obligation of that engagement, it so nearly concerning their lives. Having been some time wavering in their minds, they at last reflected on the straits they had brought themselves into, and that now they must either fight resolutely, or die; for no quarter could be expected from an enemy on whom they had committed so many cruelties.

Hereupon they encouraged one another, resolving to conquer, or spend the last drop of blood. Then they divided themselves into three battalions, sending before two hundred bucaniers, who were very dextrous at their guns. Then descending the hill, they marched directly towards the Spaniards, who in a spacious field waited for their coming. As soon as they drew nigh, the Spaniards began to shout and cry, "Viva el rey!" "God save the king!" and immediately their horse moved against the pirates: but the fields being full of quags, and soft underfoot, they could not wheel about as they desired. The two hundred bucaniers, who went before, each putting one knee to the ground, began the battle briskly, with a full volley of shot: the Spaniards defended themselves courageously, doing all they could to disorder the pirates. Their foot endeavoured to second the horse, but were constrained by the pirates to leave them. Finding themselves baffled, they attempted to drive the bulls against them behind, to put them into disorder; but the wild cattle ran away, frighted with the noise of the battle; only some few broke through the English companies, and only tore the colours in pieces, while the bucaniers shot every one of them dead.

The battle having continued two hours, the greatest part of the Spanish horse was ruined, and almost all killed: the rest fled, which the foot seeing, and that they could not possibly prevail, they discharged the shot they had in their muskets, and throwing them down, fled away, every one as he could. The pirates could not follow them, being too much harassed and wearied with their long journey. Many, not being able to fly whither they desired, hid themselves, for that present, among the shrubs of the sea-side, but very unfortunately; for most of them being found by the pirates, were instantly killed, without any quarter. Some religious men were brought prisoners before Captain Morgan; but he, being deaf to their cries, commanded them all to be pistolled, which was done. Soon after they brought a captain to him, whom he examined very strictly; particularly, wherein consisted the forces of those of Panama? He answered, their whole strength consisted in four hundred horse, twenty-four companies of foot, each of one hundred men complete; sixty Indians, and some negroes, who were to drive two thousand wild bulls upon the English, and thus, by breaking their files, put them into a total disorder: beside, that in the city they had made trenches, and raised batteries in several places, in all which they had placed many guns; and that at the entry of the highway, leading to the city, they had built a fort mounted with eight great brass guns, defended by fifty men.

Captain Morgan having heard this, gave orders instantly to march another way; but first he made a review of his men, whereof he found both killed and wounded a considerable number, and much greater than had been believed. Of the Spaniards were found six hundred dead on the place, besides the wounded and prisoners. The pirates, nothing discouraged, seeing their number so diminished, but rather filled with greater pride, perceiving what huge advantage they had obtained against their enemies, having rested some time, prepared to march courageously towards the city, plighting their oaths to one another, that they would fight till not a man was left alive. With this courage they recommenced their march, either to conquer or be conquered; carrying with them all the prisoners.

They found much difficulty in their approach to the city, for within the town the Spaniards had placed many great guns, at several quarters, some charged with small pieces of iron, and others with musket bullets; with all these they saluted the pirates at their approaching, and gave them full and frequent broadsides, firing at them incessantly; so that unavoidably they lost at every step great numbers of men. But these manifest dangers of their lives, nor the sight of so many as dropped continually at their sides, could deter them from advancing, and gaining ground every moment on the enemy; and though the Spaniards never ceased to fire, and act the best they could for their defence, yet they were forced to yield, after three hours' combat. And the pirates having possessed themselves, killed and destroyed all that attempted in the least to oppose them. The inhabitants had transported the best of their goods to more remote and occult places; howbeit, they found in the city several warehouses well stocked with merchandise, as well silks and cloths, as linen and other things of value. As soon as the first fury of their entrance was over, Captain Morgan assembled his men, and commanded them, under great penalties, not to drink or taste any wine; and the reason he gave for it was, because he had intelligence that it was all poisoned by the Spaniards. Howbeit, it was thought he gave these prudent orders to prevent the debauchery of his people, which he foresaw would be very great at the first, after so much hunger sustained by the way; fearing, withal, lest the Spaniards, seeing them in wine, should rally, and, falling on the city, use them as inhumanly as they had used the inhabitants before.

Chapter XVIII

Captain Morgan sends canoes and boats to the South Sea—He fires the city of Panama—Robberies and cruelties committed there by the pirates, till their return to the Castle of Chagre.

CAPTAIN MORGAN, as soon as he had placed necessary guards at several quarters within and without the city, commanded twenty-five men to seize a great boat, which had stuck in the mud of the port, for want of water, at a low tide. The same day about noon, he caused fire privately to be set to several great edifices of the city, nobody knowing who were the authors thereof, much less on what motives Captain Morgan did it, which are unknown to this day: the fire increased so, that before night the greatest part of the city was in a flame. Captain Morgan pretended the Spaniards had done it, perceiving that his own people reflected on him for that action. Many of the Spaniards, and some of the pirates, did what they could, either to quench the flame, or, by blowing up houses with gunpowder, and pulling down others, to stop it, but in vain: for in less than half an hour it consumed a whole street. All the houses of the city were built with cedar, very curious and magnificent, and richly adorned, especially with hangings and paintings, whereof part were before removed, and another great part were consumed by fire.

There were in this city (which is the see of a bishop) eight monasteries, seven for men, and one for women; two stately churches, and one hospital. The churches and monasteries were all richly adorned with altar-pieces and paintings, much gold and silver, and other precious things, all which the ecclesiastics had hidden. Besides which, here were two thousand houses of magnificent building, the greatest part inhabited by merchants vastly rich. For the rest of less quality, and tradesmen, this city contained five thousand more. Here were also many stables for the horses and mules that carry the plate of the king of Spain, as well as private men, towards the North Sea. The neighbouring fields are full of fertile plantations and pleasant gardens, affording delicious prospects to the inhabitants all the year.

The Genoese had in this city a stately house for their trade of negroes. This likewise was by Captain Morgan burnt to the very ground. Besides which building, there were consumed two hundred warehouses, and many slaves, who had hid themselves therein, with innumerable sacks of meal; the fire of which continued four weeks after it had begun. The greatest part of the pirates still encamped without the city, fearing and expecting the Spaniards would come and fight them anew, it being known they much outnumbered the pirates. This made them keep the field, to preserve their forces united, now much diminished by their losses. Their wounded, which were many, they put into one church, which remained standing, the rest being consumed by the fire. Besides these decreases of their men, Captain Morgan had sent a convoy of one hundred and fifty men to the castle of Chagre, to carry the news of his victory at Panama.

They saw often whole troops of Spaniards run to and fro in the fields, which made them suspect their rallying, which they never had the courage to do. In the afternoon Captain Morgan re-entered the city with his troops, that every one might take up their lodgings, which now they could hardly find, few houses having escaped the fire. Then they sought very carefully among the ruins and ashes, for utensils of plate or gold, that were not quite wasted by the flames: and of such they found no small number, especially in wells and cisterns, where the Spaniards had hid them.

Next day Captain Morgan dispatched away two troops, of one hundred and fifty men each, stout and well armed, to seek for the inhabitants who were escaped. These having made several excursions up and down the fields, woods, and mountains adjacent, returned after two days, bringing above two hundred prisoners, men, women, and slaves. The same day returned also the boat which Captain Morgan had sent to the South Sea, bringing three other boats which they had taken. But all these prizes they could willingly have given, and greater labour into the bargain, for one galleon, which miraculously escaped, richly laden with all the king's plate, jewels, and other precious goods of the best and richest merchants of Panama: on board which were also the religious women of the nunnery, who had embarked with them all the ornaments of their church, consisting in much gold, plate, and other things of great value.

The strength of this galleon was inconsiderable, having only seven guns, and ten or twelve muskets, and very ill provided with victuals, necessaries, and fresh water, having no more sails than the uppermost of the mainmast. This account the pirates received from some one who had spoken with seven mariners belonging to the galleon, who came ashore in the cockboat for fresh water. Hence they concluded they might easily have taken it, had they given her chase, as they should have done; but they were impeded from following this vastly rich prize, by their gluttony and drunkenness, having plentifully debauched themselves with several rich wines they found ready, choosing rather to satiate their appetites than to lay hold on such huge advantage; since this only prize would have been of far greater value than all they got at Panama, and the places thereabout. Next day, repenting of their negligence, being weary of their vices and debaucheries, they set forth another boat, well armed, to pursue with all speed the said galleon; but in vain, the Spaniards who were on board having had intelligence of their own danger one or two days before, while the pirates were cruising so near them; whereupon they fled to places more remote and unknown.

The pirates found, in the ports of the island of Tavoga and Tavogilla, several boats laden with very good merchandise; all which they took, and brought to Panama, where they made an exact relation of all that had passed to Captain Morgan. The prisoners confirmed what the pirates said, adding, that they undoubtedly knew where the galleon might then be, but that it was very probable they had been relieved before now from other places. This stirred up Captain Morgan anew, to send forth all the boats in the port of Panama to seek the said galleon till they could find her. These boats, being in all four, after eight days' cruising to and fro, and searching several ports and creeks, lost all hopes of finding her: hereupon they returned to Tavoga and Tavogilla; here they found a reasonable good ship newly come from Payta, laden with cloth, soap, sugar, and biscuit, with 20,000 pieces of eight; this they instantly seized, without the least resistance; as also a boat which was not far off, on which they laded great part of the merchandises from the ship, with some slaves. With this purchase they returned to Panama, somewhat better satisfied; yet, withal, much discontented that they could not meet with the galleon.

The convoy which Captain Morgan had sent to the castle of Chagre returned much about the same time, bringing with them very good news; for while Captain Morgan was on his journey to Panama, those he had left in the castle of Chagre had sent for two boats to cruise. These met with a Spanish ship, which they chased within sight of the castle. This being perceived by the pirates in the castle, they put forth Spanish colours, to deceive the ship that fled before the boats; and the poor Spaniards, thinking to take refuge under the castle, were caught in a snare, and made prisoners. The cargo on board the said vessel consisted in victuals and provisions, than which nothing could be more opportune for the castle, where they began already to want things of this kind.

This good luck of those of Chagre caused Captain Morgan to stay longer at Panama, ordering several new excursions into the country round about; and while the pirates at Panama were upon these expeditions, those at Chagre were busy in piracies on the North Sea. Captain Morgan sent forth, daily, parties of two hundred men, to make inroads into all the country round about; and when one party came back, another went forth, who soon gathered much riches, and many prisoners. These being brought into the city, were put to the most exquisite tortures, to make them confess both other people's goods and their own. Here it happened that one poor wretch was found in the house of a person of quality, who had put on, amidst the confusion, a pair of taffety breeches of his master's, with a little silver key hanging out; perceiving which, they asked him for the cabinet of the said key. His answer was, he knew not what was become of it, but that finding those breeches in his master's house, he had made bold to wear them. Not being able to get any other answer, they put him on the rack, and inhumanly disjointed his arms; then they twisted a cord about his forehead, which they wrung so hard that his eyes appeared as big as eggs, and were ready to fall out. But with these torments not obtaining any positive answer, they hung him up by the wrists, giving him many blows and stripes under that intolerable pain and posture of body. Afterwards they cut off his nose and ears, and singed his face with burning straw, till he could not speak, nor lament his misery any longer: then, losing all hopes of any confession, they bade a negro run him through, which put an end to his life, and to their inhuman tortures. Thus did many others of those miserable prisoners finish their days, the common sport and recreation of these pirates being such tragedies.

Captain Morgan having now been at Panama full three weeks, commanded all things to be prepared for his departure. He ordered every company of men to seek so many beasts of carriage as might convey the spoil to the river where his canoes lay. About this time there was a great rumour, that a considerable number of pirates intended to leave Captain Morgan; and that, taking a ship then in port, they determined to go and rob on the South Sea, till they had got as much as they thought fit, and then return homewards, by way of the East Indies. For which purpose they had gathered much provisions, which they had hid in private places, with sufficient powder, bullets, and all other ammunition: likewise some great guns belonging to the town, muskets, and other things, wherewith they designed not only to equip their vessel, but to fortify themselves in some island which might serve them for a place of refuge.

This design had certainly taken effect, had not Captain Morgan had timely advice of it from one of their comrades: hereupon he commanded the mainmast of the said ship to be cut down and burnt, with all the other boats in the port: hereby the intentions of all or most of his companions were totally frustrated. Then Captain Morgan sent many of the Spaniards into the adjoining fields and country to seek for money, to ransom not only themselves, but the rest of the prisoners, as likewise the ecclesiastics. Moreover, he commanded all the artillery of the town to be nailed and stopped up. At the same time he sent out a strong company of men to seek for the governor of Panama, of whom intelligence was brought, that he had laid several ambuscades in the way by which he ought to return: but they returned soon after, saying they had not found any sign of any such ambuscades. For confirmation whereof, they brought some prisoners, who declared that the said governor had had an intention of making some opposition by the way, but that the men designed to effect it were unwilling to undertake it: so that for want of means he could not put his design in execution.

February 24, 1671, Captain Morgan departed from Panama, or rather from the place where the city of Panama stood; of the spoils whereof he carried with him one hundred and seventy-five beasts of carriage, laden with silver, gold, and other precious things, beside about six hundred prisoners, men, women, children and slaves. That day they came to a river that passes through a delicious plain, a league from Panama: here Captain Morgan put all his forces into good order, so as that the prisoners were in the middle, surrounded on all sides with pirates, where nothing else was to be heard but lamentations, cries, shrieks, and doleful sighs of so many women and children, who feared Captain Morgan designed to transport them all into his own country for slaves. Besides, all those miserable prisoners endured extreme hunger and thirst at that time, which misery Captain Morgan designedly caused them to sustain, to excite them to seek for money to ransom themselves, according to the tax he had set upon every one. Many of the women begged Captain Morgan, on their knees, with infinite sighs and tears, to let them return to Panama, there to live with their dear husbands and children in little huts of straw, which they would erect, seeing they had no houses till the rebuilding of the city. But his answer was, "He came not thither to hear lamentations and cries, but to seek money: therefore they ought first to seek out that, wherever it was to be had, and bring it to him; otherwise he would assuredly transport them all to such places whither they cared not to go."

Next day, when the march began, those lamentable cries and shrieks were renewed, so as it would have caused compassion in the hardest heart: but Captain Morgan, as a man little given to mercy, was not moved in the least. They marched in the same order as before, one party of the pirates in the van, the prisoners in the middle, and the rest of the pirates in the rear; by whom the miserable Spaniards were at every step punched and thrust in their backs and sides, with the blunt ends of their arms, to make them march faster.

A beautiful lady, wife to one of the richest merchants of Tavoga, was led prisoner by herself, between two pirates. Her lamentations pierced the skies, seeing herself carried away into captivity often crying to the pirates, and telling them, "That she had given orders to two religious persons, in whom she had relied, to go to a certain place, and fetch so much money as her ransom did amount to; that they had promised faithfully to do it, but having obtained the money, instead of bringing it to her, they had employed it another way, to ransom some of their own, and particular friends." This ill action of theirs was discovered by a slave, who brought a letter to the said lady. Her complaints, and the cause thereof, being brought to Captain Morgan, he thought fit to inquire thereinto. Having found it to be true— especially hearing it confirmed by the confession of the said religious men, though under some frivolous exercises of having diverted the money but for a day or two, in which time they expected more sums to repay it—he gave liberty to the said lady, whom otherwise he designed to transport to Jamaica. But he detained the said religious men as prisoners in her place, using them according to their deserts.

Captain Morgan arriving at the town called Cruz, on the banks of the river Chagre, he published an order among the prisoners, that within three days every one should bring in their ransom, under the penalty of being transported to Jamaica. Meanwhile he gave orders for so much rice and maize to be collected thereabouts, as was necessary for victualling his ships. Here some of the prisoners were ransomed, but many others could not bring in their money. Hereupon he continued his voyage, leaving the village on the 5th of March following, carrying with him all the spoil he could. Hence he likewise led away some new prisoners, inhabitants there, with those in Panama, who had not paid their ransoms. But the two religious men, who had diverted the lady's money, were ransomed three days after by other persons, who had more compassion for them than they had showed for her.

About the middle of the way to Chagre, Captain Morgan commanded them to be mustered, and caused every one to be sworn, that they had concealed nothing, even not to the value of sixpence. This done, Captain Morgan knowing those lewd fellows would not stick to swear falsely for interest, he commanded every one to be searched very strictly, both in their clothes and satchels, and elsewhere. Yea, that this order might not be ill taken by his companions, he permitted himself to be searched, even to his very shoes. To this effect, by common consent, one was assigned out of every company to be searchers of the rest. The French pirates that assisted on this expedition disliked this new practice of searching; but, being outnumbered by the English, they were forced to submit as well as the rest. The search being over, they re-embarked, and arrived at the castle of Chagre on the 9th of March. Here they found all things in good order, excepting the wounded men whom they had left at their departure; for of these the greatest number were dead of their wounds.

From Chagre, Captain Morgan sent, presently after his arrival, a great boat to Puerto Bello, with all the prisoners taken at the isle of St. Catherine, demanding of them a considerable ransom for the castle of Chagre, where he then was; threatening otherwise to ruin it. To this those of Puerto Bello answered, they would not give one farthing towards the ransom of the said castle, and the English might do with it as they pleased. Hereupon the dividend was made of all the spoil made in that voyage; every company, and every particular person therein, receiving their proportion, or rather what part thereof Captain Morgan pleased to give them. For the rest of his companions, even of his own nation, murmured at his proceedings, and told him to his face that he had reserved the best jewels to himself: for they judged it impossible that no greater share should belong to them than two hundred pieces of eight, per capita, of so many valuable plunders they had made; which small sum they thought too little for so much labour, and such dangers, as they had been exposed to. But Captain Morgan was deaf to all this, and many other like complaints, having designed to cheat them of what he could.

At last, finding himself obnoxious to many censures of his people, and fearing the consequence, he thought it unsafe to stay any longer at Chagre, but ordered the ordnance of the castle to be carried on board his ship; then he caused most of the walls to be demolished, the edifices to be burnt, and as many other things ruined as could be done in a short time. This done, he went secretly on board his own ship, without giving any notice to his companions, and put out to sea, being only followed by three or four vessels of the whole fleet. These were such (as the French pirates believed) as went shares with Captain Morgan in the best part of the spoil, which had been concealed from them in the dividend. The Frenchmen could willingly have revenged themselves on Captain Morgan and his followers, had they been able to encounter him at sea; but they were destitute of necessaries, and had much ado to find sufficient provisions for their voyage to Jamaica, he having left them unprovided for all things.

Made in the USA
San Bernardino, CA
29 November 2019